D1247550

Under the Fig Tree

PALESTINIAN STORIES BY

YITZHAK SHENBERG

SCHOCKEN BOOKS / NEW YORK

TRANSLATED FROM THE HEBREW BY I. M. LASK

CONTENTS

71-841

UNDER THE FIG TREE

HAKHAM NEHEMIAH PARSI was blind in one eye. The folk of the quarter said that many years before, he had happened to be sleeping out in the open when a night bird came along and pecked out his eye; but the vision in his remaining eye had increased, so that he could look ahead and foresee what was going to happen. Ever since his accident people had been asking him to tell their fortune. Men and women, boys and girls, all came and sat fearfully trembling in his presence, anxiously awaiting his word. Hakham Nehemiah used to fix them with his seeing eye, the whole of which bespoke severity. He would look deep into the hearts and innermost thoughts of all, and reveal their life stories. Never did he conceal a man's fate, or pityingly make it more easy to bear. All that he foresaw he would tell, "from almond rod to seething pot." One might have supposed that whatever compassion he had, had shrunk into the blind eye stuck in his overcast face, whose lashes quivered as though seeking an outlet for their enclosed tears.

Hakham Nehemiah kept to himself and never left his home save for prayer with the congregation. He was habitually silent, sitting most of the time on the mat in his room down in the dark cellar, his crossed hands inside his sleeves, and his head to one

9

side. It was only when he began to tell fortunes that his voice would suddenly bloom. His tongue would burst into metaphor and every word would be melodious and pleasant.

His method of telling a fortune was most singular. A wooden tray lay before him on the mat, and to the right of it was a little box of sand. On the tray he would incline a white sieve, and strew seven handfuls of sand over the sieve. The sand sifting through would pile up in tiny heaps on the tray below. Hakham Nehemiah would gaze at the windings and markings between the heaps and order the person who had come to hear his fortune to run his finger through the web of sand at random. Only then would the Hakham begin relating what was concealed in the womb of the future; and he would speak with confidence as though he were reading from a book. At first he used to take one piaster, but as more and more people flocked to his door, he raised his rate to two piasters and sometimes to as much as half a shilling.

Hakham Nehemiah was a widower. His oldest son had wandered off to distant places and had got as far as South America. His second son was a peddler who made the rounds of Ishmaelite villages and earned a scanty living for his own household. There was nobody left with Hakham Nehemiah except his daughter Esther, a dark girl of about seventeen with two thick plaits hanging down her back. In the daytime she busied herself in the cellar, edged her way between the stalls in the market place to buy food cheap, prepared food for her father, and washed his clothes. When evening fell she would join her friends, of whom a few were pupils at the school of the *Alliance,* while most of them worked in Ashkenazic households; she would listen to tales of the manner in which Ashkenazic Jews lived and their luxurious ways.

She herself had never attended any school nor had she ever left Jerusalem; and when she asked permission to go out into service like her friends, her father forbade her to do any such thing, for it was not in accordance with his honor and breeding.

Esther was afraid of her father, and she feared his silence even more than she trembled at his words. Whenever she heard him in the neighboring room, telling a fortune and chanting his metaphors, it seemed to her that a veil had been raised in the corner and that there was something lurking there which was neither fish nor fowl; something as yet unborn. Above all, her heart would leap up when she saw her father sitting alone sifting the sand through the sieve, gazing motionless at the tiny mounds on the tray, blowing at them, blurring the markings, and sifting the sand all over again. At such times it seemed to her as though he were vainly telling the fortunes of the nameless ones who were still to be created; as one who amuses himself by building worlds of sand and then destroying them.

A few weeks after her mother had died, when the very house grew lonely and orphaned, Esther placed herself in front of her father, began plucking at the end of her plait, cast her eyes to the ground, and said: "Tell me my fortune, too, *ya-abba.*"

Hakham Nehemiah looked at her with his open eye, the lashes of his blind eye quivered and he remained silent for a little while. Then he shook his head and said: "No, I shall not tell it to you."

11

She turned away with shaking knees and left him, her heart heaving and her spirit depressed. She went out and sat on the stone step at the entrance to the cellar, while in front of her curled the gray cat, blinking his eyes and purring all inside him. For a long while she sat thinking of her father who would tell anyone's fortune for a copper; but not that of his only daughter, who had grown up. Again and again she wondered whether he feared that he might see trouble and distress ahead of her; or whether he had no faith in his own forecasting. After some time had passed she went to him again and said: "*Ya-abba*, you tell everybody's fortune. Will you not show me what is to come? Why should I go on groping in the dark?"

But Hakham rebuked her hoarsely: "Go away, go. I shall not tell it to you. I shall make your fortune for you myself. With my own hands I shall make it."

When Esther saw that she could get nothing from him, she thought matters over and in the evening, while her father was in the House of Prayer, she went up to the sand-box and set out to tell her own fortune. With trembling hands she sifted the handfuls of sand through the sieve, and bent down over the little piles heaped up on the tray; but she could distinguish nothing. She moved her finger to make the furrow of her fortune in the approved fashion, but the gray cat lying in the dark corner suddenly jumped up, walked across the sand and blurred all the markings. Esther shuddered, swept all the sand back into the box and hurried away. For a long time afterward her heart beat hard because of what had happened.

Hakham Nehemiah had some renown in the quarter, but his honor and glory waxed sevenfold from
the time folk saw Shelomo Aridi paying him a visit.
Aridi was a man of about fifty-five, short and fleshy,
with a thick nose, pouting lips, and a gold chain
hanging across his paunch. He had come to Jerusalem from Turkestan without kinsmen or family,
but with a large amount of money; nobody knew
what his calling had been in the country of his ori-
gin, or where he had obtained his wealth. Upon his
arrival he purchased a spacious house with numer-
ous rooms in the Bet Yaakov Quarter, deposited the
balance of his money in various banks and lived an
idle, solitary and quiet life.

When Aridi came to visit Hakham Nehemiah, the
latter was astonished at the honor and rose to receive him. They sat facing one another; Hakham
Nehemiah found it hard to inquire immediately
what the visitor desired, so he began to engage him
in conversation on local and worldly affairs. After
a little while, though, Aridi began to tug at the tip
of his beard, lowered his eyes and said: "I have come
to you, Hakham Nehemiah, for you to tell me my
fortune, too."

"Fortune?" smiled Hakham Nehemiah in astonishment.

"Yes, for you know, 'the sea is never full' and the
heart can never be filled. A man has to know the
course of his life. Not that I wish to make inquiry,
God forbid, about the final disposition of all things;
merely the smallest part, a tiny fragment will be
enough. Here I am pushing along from one day to

the next, and the candle burns until it gutters. And what then? No good! My house is at peace and I have no cause for fear, yet I know no quiet within me. I go my way lonely and there is no joy in my dwelling; and that is not good. So I decided to look around for someone, and I found a widow-woman. Maybe you know her? Her name is Rivkah Hadjar. She is a fit and proper woman who knows how to conduct a household and is careful in her ways. Now I have come for you to favor me with a word, and to see what will happen with me and her."

Hakham Nehemiah listened attentively. His hands, concealed in their sleeves, fidgeted a little in their hiding place, like two whelps pushing to get out. His open eye resumed its severity, while the blinded one began to twitch as usual. He withdrew his hands from their hiding place, took the sieve, inclined it in front of him and began scattering sand upon it from the box. On the tray there rapidly began to appear small soft heaps, like rounded thighs, or twining vine tendrils; and fortune engraved its utterance in a runic script of marks and tittles and traces for the eye to decipher. Then Hakham Nehemiah signaled to Aridi, who passed his short finger through the sand, running his furrow across it. Hakham Nehemiah crouched, holding his breath, and stared.

"Widow?" said he in a low voice. "I see nothing like that. No widow has been allotted to you, *mari*, my master."

"No?" exclaimed Aridi in astonishment, shaking his head. "How can that be? I thought she was!"

"I can see nothing of what you tell me."

14

"I had the idea that this woman and I were particularly suited for one another. A widow still in her best years, still fresh, and who in spite of that will not be spoiled, and will not shame me. To be sure, she has a lad of about fifteen, but I had thought to provide for him one way or another and be rid of him. Then I would have a wife who would be all mine, who would think me the crown of her head and bring me pleasure."

"No, *mari*, as I see it, there is a virgin maiden waiting for you. A modest and pious girl who keeps the straight and narrow path, who watches the vineyard of her body, wearing shame like a cloak, her body fashioned and her limbs perfect and her spirit humble and all of her a hidden treasure."

Hakham Nehemiah spoke in a slow chant, and Aridi listened to his words as though under a spell. "A virgin maiden?" he asked in a whisper, as though dreaming. "Yet I have many years behind me, Hakham Nehemiah."

"Who and what am I? I cannot say whether this is evil or whether it is good, but only that it is your fortune; that I tell you, and nothing more. I have neither hand nor part in this."

"Surely, surely, Hakham Nehemiah," murmured Aridi to calm him down. "It is a matter of general knowledge that the Holy One, blessed be he, has given you a portion of the Higher Understanding. Still what you say astonishes me, for in my heart I have been thinking that I am by now poor in spirit, an ox bound to the furrow, and that I would no longer seek the meadows."

"The thoughts of the heart are as rising dust, but

15

fortune shows things moving in their courses. Assuredly He who giveth the weary strength will give vigor to those that have no might."

"And can you see there who she is and what she is?"

"I see a poor girl of good family. And I also see a life of sweetness and heart's ease and joyful faces, an Eden full of delight and tenderness."

"May God bless you, Hakham Nehemiah," said Aridi very quietly. "And do you see children?"

"A woman I see, and round her sons three."

"Three!" Aridi started, slapping his thigh with satisfaction. "Indeed, indeed, I never dreamed of that!" He quieted down a little, and said: "And are there no signs to tell us which of the girls in the quarter it can be? Maybe, God forbid, it is the daughter of Asali? Why, she runs about with lads and goes to illicit places, and is impudent, and her ways are crooked. Or maybe the daughter of *Mari* Yehia, but she has sore eyes and no breasts at all!"

Hakham Nehemiah blew on the strewn sand, covered over the mysterious cryptic writing, looked at him once again and said:

"If this is the decree of fortune, you have no reason for concern. Only keep your eyes open as you go, and she will be discovered unto you."

Aridi left dazed and excited, full of many thoughts. When he reached the door, he saw Esther sitting on the stone step, her two heavy plaits hanging down her back. Confused, he came to a standstill before her. His mouth suddenly opened; the spaces between his yellow teeth filled with saliva. He stood stock-still, gazing and smiling until the girl blushed and ran away.

When Aridi's go-between came to suggest his marriage with Esther, Hakham Nehemiah received him calmly and without any expression, just as though he had been sure from the first that this would come about, and so had no reason to be astonished. He sat as usual with his legs crossed and his hands hidden in his sleeves, while his son the peddler, who happened to be visiting him, stood respectfully. The messenger coughed once and then again and started to speak carefully and in roundabout fashion, beginning by talking of the decline of the younger generation and the excellent qualities to be found in a man of experience. Then, like a man of the world, he began to go into details about all the riches of the world, and finally cleverly introduced the name of Aridi and started to tell tales of all the business he had with banks and of his status and his magnificent home.

Hakham Nehemiah listened silently, not making the slightest movement, although his son impatiently shifted from foot to foot. When the man stopped talking, Hakham Nehemiah replied briefly: "Master Shelomo has done us honor, and our heart is as full as the sea with gratitude. But we must consider the matter, and it is also necessary to ask the girl."

No sooner had the messenger left the house than Esther burst out of the kitchen and fell at her father's feet: "What is this you are doing to me, *ya-abba*? What have you thought up for me? The world is large and there is a father in heaven. Is this the fortune you are making for me with your own hands?"

Hakham Nehemiah turned his head to her and his blind eye twitched. "You will be a wealthy lady," he began with his high-flown speech, as was his way when he sat crouching over the sands of fortune. "You will be a great lady and wear a crown of jewels, the girls will envy you and all the women of the quarter will seek your friendship. You will have a house with magnificent furniture, you will wear splendid dresses and go forth in precious stones, and you will have money in your purse and no longer need to count every penny. Whether you wish it for charity or for women's finery—you will receive it all the same. You will deck your couch with coverlets, my daughter, you will no longer toil, and every day will be a delight. I have strewn you a glorious fortune, that you may enjoy the fat of the land."

His son supported him, mumbling in a low voice, "And the food they will put on your table! And how you will be respected by the whole neighborhood! We shall all be blessed through you, and your star will give light to all our family!"

Esther lay on the mat, her face covered with her hands, sobbing quietly. Through her tears she asked between her fingers: "And you, *ya-abba*, what will you do without me? How will you get along, alone and forsaken? Who will cook your food for you, and who will wash your things? It will be terrible for you, terrible! Let me stay with you, I shall be the shadow at your right hand, I shall walk about on the tips of my toes and you will not notice me, I shall close my mouth and you will not hear me.

18

Let me stay, *ya-abba!*"

Hakham Nehemiah remained silent and shook his head, as though he were still chanting to himself. But the peddler brother pushed Esther slightly with his foot and said: "Get up, pick yourself up! What reason have you to be shedding such foolish tears! You don't know what is good for you, and what heaven is offering you. Here you are, told to dress up to enter a fine house, and you cry! They tell you you can make yourself clothes of fine linen and silks, of satin and velvet—and you shed tears! Think a little! Gather whatever sense you have in your head, and do a little thinking. And don't worry about father. My daughter Hannah will be ten years old in a little while, and she can come here every day to serve father. And now get up!"

Esther rose to her feet and looked around her with wondering eyes. She saw the dark cellar in which she had spent her life, and it was far, far darker than ever before.

[IV]

When the time for the wedding drew near, Esther gathered her scanty belongings together, bundled them in a red kerchief she had inherited from her mother and went to stay with her aunt in a distant courtyard. For Esther held that a wedding needs a woman's hand, and since she had no mother it would be good to have the support of her aunt, who was well versed in the customs and ceremonies of weddings.

Aridi sent many betrothal gifts to his bride, all of them sensible things made to last a long time;

19

as though Esther was another kind of bank, where he could deposit part of his wealth. "By reason of the mourning for Zion," if one may apply the expression, the wedding took place without any fuss. The table groaned under the food and the guests gave vent to deep belches, but the occasion was not completely a joyous one. The bridegroom himself maintained his gravity and refrained from demonstrating any youthful enthusiasm. He invited no musicians or jesters to the feast, and when the womenfolk wished to raise their voices in the bride's room in a succession of throaty flourishes, he waved his hands for silence. Instead he gave freely to charity, though in moderation and accounting for every penny, and the beggars who crowded round the house grumbled darkly. "Let him pay, let the old reprobate pay! It does not matter, such a turtle dove has fallen to his lot—he ought to pay properly!"

The day after the wedding a vast silence descended upon Aridi's house. No window was opened, no curtain moved, no door creaked, as though the whole world were silent and still; and only Simha the old servant woman went about her household affairs. After a week had passed, the door opened wide, and Aridi came to the threshold and yawned long and loud into the air. The household returned to its former lazy habits. Esther disturbed them only for a little while, and was quickly provided with her place in the daily round; one of silence and boredom. All morning long Aridi used to walk about the rooms, wrapped in a wide dressing gown with untied girdle, and his paunch bulging like a ball, while he fingered the string of coral beads in his hand and cracked sunflower seeds between his teeth.

After his noon nap he would put on his blue suit and go downtown to spend some time with the businessmen.

He did not allow Esther to go out. She could not even pay a visit to her father's house, but was required to eat and drink and fatten herself up properly. Only on the Sabbath evenings would he take her out for a walk on the new highway in front of the quarter. He would walk ahead with his hands clasped behind him, while Esther stepped slowly after him, teetering on her high heels and looking down at the ground. The girls of the quarter used to look in her direction, and whispered enviously together about her black silk dress, the red linen rose in her bosom, the rings on her fingers and the bracelets on her arms. But when they returned home Aridi would take the jewelry off his wife, and lock it away in the heavy, ironbound box. Esther would once again sit down to her endless embroidering, and her husband would once again put on his dressing gown, and walk around the house, slapping about in his heelless slippers, coughing and snorting and waiting for her to bear him a son.

After a few weeks had passed he began to look at her with an impatient question, passing his hands over her to see if she had any "joy from the womb," until Esther would blush and fly from him into another room. When several months had passed and Aridi saw that his hope must be deferred, he began to lose patience. Sometimes he would disturb the calm of the house, jumping up in the middle of the day to berate Esther with:

"All she has inside her is a feeding trough! Oh, what a misfortune! Oh, what have I brought into my house! She had nothing but the hair on her head when I married her, and now she is as barren as a rock, as sterile as a thornbush in the field! I thought I was fattening a heifer, but she is nothing but a stubborn she-mule! She just won't hold it! Oh! Oh! A black life, a life of trouble! A whole year and nothing to show. A fine year gone to the Dead Sea! O you fool, you fool!" He would beat his chest. "You have bought a wick for a copper, and thought to make it a candelabrum! What's the matter? Oh, God bless your father for having done me this kindness!"

Hakham Nehemiah and his son the peddler sometimes used to visit Esther for coffee. They would sit shyly in a corner, enjoying the handsome room. On a few occasions Hakham Nehemiah received money gifts from his son-in-law, and on festival days he would come and eat at his table. His son also endeavored to become friendly with his brother-in-law and to ask him for a loan, but Aridi pushed out his underlip, screwed up his thick nose, and shook his head over the expenses that were fairly eating up his capital, and finally sent him away empty-handed.

When Hakham Nehemiah came to see his daughter on such a day of anger, Aridi stationed himself before him, placed his hands on his hips, and said: "And when will that sign come, Hakham Nehemiah? You said something about a sign; when will it happen?"

"What, what?" stammered the Hakham, and the cup of coffee froze in his hand halfway to his mouth.

"When I came to you the first time, what did you tell me? You promised something definite, I remember. I heard it with my own ears. And what now?"

Hakham Nehemiah recovered himself and thought it over. "God will be merciful," said he, as he calmly sipped his coffee.

"Yes, but when, when? Am I Methuselah or Father Abraham? What do you suppose I am? Are you telling me to hope for miracles? Look, a year has passed and there is no sign. I wanted to take the widow in the first place. She is fertile, has fruit from her womb to prove it; and there could be no going wrong in her case. But you stopped me saying, Oh, no, you will have three sons!"

Hakham Nehemiah did not answer. Esther, who was sitting by the window with her hands in her lap, rose and left the room.

"Did you say three sons or did you not?" Aridi demanded again, his lips wet and his brow moist. "Can you see the future, or do you make it up from your own head! I heard you say with my own ears: three sons!"

The Hakham closed his blind eye tight, and his good eye cast its severity across his troubled face. "So I said," he responded in a low voice. "I remember too. There will be three sons in this house, I said."

"Yes, you said so, you said so!" seethed Aridi, but immediately stood stock-still, his head thrust forward and his eyes starting out of their sockets. "Oh, oh!" he choked in his throat.

That night the people of the quarter heard a shouting and wailing from the house of Aridi. Esther howled at the top of her voice, while her husband voided curses upon her. "Do you propose to inherit me? Do you expect to fling me into the grave and be left a grand lady? I shall get up and write a new will and cut you off without a single penny. You will leave as naked as when you came! I shall leave you only a single shilling to remember me by, and you can buy sunflower seeds to crack, the way you have cracked my heart!"

The women of the quarter tossed on their beds and sighed:

"Oh, oh, the poor thing, the life she has to put up with!"

Once again Aridi trumpeted into the vastness of the night: "It's sons I want, wench! What have you hung those two bags on your chest for? And what is your belly? Just a heap of muck! Just a crazy wind inside of her! Give me sons, sons!"

[v]

In the course of five years Aridi changed his will seven times, and after he had torn it up for the seventh time he had a stroke and died within three days. Since there were no heirs to be found, Esther inherited all his property. She gave part of the money to her brother, who opened a grocery shop, and distributed various amounts among her father and her other kinsfolk and among charitable institutions. She herself stayed on in the spacious house, together with Simha; and she spent her time in embroidery and knitting, as was her wont. Her house became full of unnecessary table napkins, pieces of lace and fringes; her days passed slowly, too, like a purposeless embroidery. As before, she did not visit her father's house, but Hakham Nehemiah used to come to see her from time to time, and sitting at his ease drinking his coffee, he would say:

"Be at ease, my daughter, be at ease for a while. The temporary knot has been cut, but with the aid of God you will merit an everlasting knot in its place. You still have good years to come, God helping, and you shall yet wear a garland of roses that will never be scattered. Relax, my daughter."

"I am at ease, *ya-abba*, I am resting," Esther would answer him in her soft voice, but by now she could pluck up enough courage to gaze directly into both her father's eyes, the good and the blind, fearlessly. As she sat facing him it seemed to her that a heavy tear was gathering in her and blinding one of her own eyes, while the other's sight was being doubled. But that eye could not range into the future; instead, for a moment it saw deep into her very soul, saw tiny creatures crawling in the dark, creatures formless and nameless. Then she would start back at the sight her own self, clasp her hands together and repeat:

"I am at ease, *ya-abba*, I am at ease."

In due course, busybody women began to visit her, wearing cheerful faces, passing broad hints which left very little implied; but Esther paid them no attention. She felt no stirrings within her, and did not regard herself as a released prisoner. She merely sat silent, joining hours of contemplation to hours of boredom, all of her like a garden shut up and a fountain sealed.

If she had any thoughts, they were about the widow Rivkah Hadjar. Now, she would say to herself, we are both widows. She has a son and I have a house; but could one strike a balance and find out which of us has received the more bitter portion from the Almighty?

She had never seen Rivkah Hadjar in her life,

nor did she know whether the latter had ever heard that Aridi had been intending to marry her. But in the twilight of her heart she always reckoned that the widow must assuredly be poverty-stricken and be cursing her young rival all the time for having robbed her of her measure of contentment in life. Doubtless in her rage she had neither rested nor remained quiet until Esther too had put on the veil of widowhood. There it is, Esther would say to herself, I have come this far. How old am I altogether? Twenty-four years old, yet a widow already, a widow already, a widow already.

[VI]

One day Esther sat as usual at the window, lazily plying her embroidery needle. It was noon, the hour when most people sit at table. Esther looked out and saw a young man standing in the shade of the tree near the fence, gazing at her and smiling. She could not make out his features, except for a gleaming that flashed in her direction; a radiant smile, white teeth, hair glistening with olive oil; and a tie the color of a peacock's tail. Dazzled, she moved away, and lowered the curtain.

At lunch-time the next day, the same fellow again appeared in the shade of the tree, and stood there for quite a while before moving on. On the third day Esther did not go to the window again, but called Simha who was busy in the kitchen, and said to her: "Simha, Simha, come and see whether he is still standing there."

Simha came in with her frying pan in her hand, wearing a sullen look. "Who? Where?" she grumbled as she looked out through the window, then added: "Oh, that's the son of the widow Hadjar!"

At that Esther thought that she would faint. She pressed her two hands to her breast and closed her eyes tight for a moment. "What is he doing here?" she asked hoarsely.

Simha did not grasp what she meant and answered: "He is a clerk in a building materials firm."

Had he found out? Esther wondered to herself. Could he know that he and his mother would have inherited the house, if Hakham Nehemiah had not married his daughter off to Aridi? Did he propo to take his revenge on her now that she had been left alone and helpless?

"Simha," she said weakly, "go out and ask him what he wants, and why he comes here to shame me in front of the whole neighborhood."

Simha grumbled something between her flabby lips and went down to the young man, while Esther stood leaning against the wall with heaving heart. A few moments later the old servant woman returned and said:

"His name is Ezra, and he says that the lamp has gone out in his heart and he wishes to kindle it once again at the light of your countenance."

There was not a spark of emotion in the dull eyes of Simha, neither curiosity nor mockery. She gazed at her mistress and waited for her to say something; but Esther remained silent and pale.

That night Esther could not sleep, but tossed about on her bed, moaning softly. She was afraid of the man and afraid of his intentions. She feared the naked laughter on his face and the veiled meanings in his words. Why had he left her alone until

27

now and ignored her? Could he have been sent from heaven as a punishment upon her for the sins she had committed against her will? Had Aridi come to him in a dream and revealed that he had first intended to marry his widowed mother? Would this man henceforward drive away her peace of mind and persecute her until she grew sick of living and maimed by misery?

Esther thought many thoughts, and they were all chilling. Yet, despite herself, a warm undercurrent flowed ceaselessly in her innermost being. When she rose in the morning she did not dare to raise the window curtain, but walked around the room restlessly, impatiently awaiting the noon hour, when the clerks went home for lunch. When she saw Hadjar through the curtain, she hurried to the kitchen, took Simha by the hand and whispered in her ear: "Simha, go down and ask him whether it is my money on which he has set his eyes."

Simha went and returned with the answer:

"He says, 'Is money a defect in a woman?'"

Esther listened with her mouth open, unable to speak. Next day she no longer waited for the noon hour, but sent Simha into the street a long time before.

"Wait for him there," said she. "Wait and say to him, 'Let me alone; perhaps you do not know that you are younger than I am.'"

Simha turned and went away with her dragging gait, to stand waiting in the street with bent head. When she came back, she said in a dull voice:

"He says, 'Is youth a blemish in a man?'"

Esther spread out her hands and with trembling knees approached the window. She pulled the curtain aside, leaned against the sill and thrust her body out, not caring whether all the people of the neighborhood saw her.

[VII]

That night Hadjar stood below Esther' open window, while she trembled above him in * ark-ness of her room.

"Go away, go away from here," she w' *red as though she were mad. "Clear off or I * shout."

"Why should you shout? I am not * *ief, but a poor beggar. The poor one uses en* *ties, and is that a reason to raise your voice an* *out?"

"What do you want of me?"

"I have come to ask you to g* back what was stolen."

"What was stolen?" Esther w* *ng her fingers, and there was a choking sensation *n her throat.

"Yes, you have stolen my peace of mind, and I demand it back."

"You are making fun of me. Even in the darkness I can see that your eyes are laughing."

"What it is in my eyes is in my soul."

Esther wished to clear up once for all the question which was oppressing her, and to tell him that she was not responsible because Aridi had not married his mother; but she could not now find the words. She leaned down to him and said, shaking her head:

"It is not me you want, but my money."

"I only pick up the rope from the ground to lead away the cow that is tied to it."

"And what did you do all these years?"

29

"I was in a hurry to grow up and grow older in order to catch up with you." Hadjar laughed up at her from below.

"But you move about among people and many pretty young girls must come your way. Why do you come to me?"

"Since when does one find a pearl among lentils?"

"Ah, ah," said Esther suppressing a sigh. "I was fast asleep and had grown accustomed to it. Why have you come to wake me up?"

"No man sleeps when the drum beats near his ear," he flashed his teeth at her again. "What is all this talk about your long sleep? You were fashioned for joy by day and pleasures by night; that is what I see in you and that is what I tell you."

"What joy? What joy, man? Can you suck honey out of rock? I am weighed down with troubles."

"Even in the king's palace there is a refuse bin."

"No, no, stop talking. I have stopped living. There is no more life in me."

" 'There are no more wells in the earth,' says the thirsty man in the desert."

She was silent for a moment, then said: "I am afraid of you."

"A wild cat found a chick and said, 'I am afraid of you,' and sank her teeth in it."

"If I could see what was going on in your inner-most heart!"

"Look into the mirror and you will see what is in my heart."

"Go away, go away from here, O pleasant one, or people will see us."

"What will they see? They will see smoke rising

from the house, and will say that bread is baking in the oven."

"Go, my darling, go, my star and the bird of my soul, do me no evil and cast no shame upon me."

"Let me hold your hand."

"Why my hand? I and all that is mine are yours. Go and send me your go-between if you still feel the same."

[VIII]

Ezra came into the silent house of Esther like a storm. The windows were flung wide open, the walls were painted afresh, furniture was added—all with the greatest haste, as though Ezra had sworn to restore to his wife, in a single moment, all that her life had been deprived of from the day she had left her father's house. Esther was overwhelmed, as though a great wave had suddenly swept down upon her and swung her up to a height from which she looked down, all but fainting with fear and happiness.

When Ezra first brought his widowed mother to meet her, the fear that Esther had felt in her heart all this time melted in a single moment. The widow Hadjar was a large-faced, broad-hipped woman, large-eyed and cheerful, her voice always hearty, always screaming in gales of laughter. As soon as she came in, she filled all the rooms with noises and echoes and a host of speeches and questions and demands. She promptly commenced a lively debate with her son, about the furniture and the household affairs, and they argued back and forth joyously and noisily, while Esther stood to one side, a smile on her lips as she silently warmed herself at their great blaze.

This time her wedding was a large affair. Following the ceremony they had many guests over to a "party" after the European style, with a gramophone and English songs and dancing and a great deal of drinking. Even after the wedding was over the old quiet did not return. The widow moved to her son's new home and began to run the household. Ezra resigned from his post and did not think of business at all, but spent any amount of money on clothes and pleasures; as though he was not yet accustomed to regarding this money as his own. Since Esther had time enough and to spare, he would regularly take her to cafés and cinemas, to parties, and visiting. All at once she learned how to walk easily and freely on high heels, and she no longer felt as if she were in fetters when she wore silks and velvets. Every day became a holiday; she was dazed and confused, and her heart was full of thanksgiving.

Nobody forced her to eat and get fat any more. On the contrary, she would be the first up in the morning and would be busy in the kitchen with Simha, preparing breakfast, which she would take back on tiptoe to Ezra and his mother. They used to eat in bed, yawning and chattering noisily, while Esther happily served them, smiling and nodding and quivering within.

She kept quivering until she conceived and bore a son.

At this point Ezra sobered up and began taking stock. He said to his wife:

"This is quite enough of a good thing. Now I have to find myself something to do."

"Do whatever you feel like doing," replied Esther.

"I have to start some sort of business of my own. I can't be another man's slave any more."

"No, *ya-habibi*, you are enthroned in my heart, so how can you serve others?"

Esther transferred her bank account to his name, and he borrowed additional money and mortgaged the house, and went into business as a building contractor. He was diligent and kept his word, and people came to like him. But, being in a hurry to strengthen his position, he began to accept contracts at cut prices and lost money.

"It does not matter," he said to comfort Esther. "The first step—you fall. My competitors are trying to keep me from expanding. But I shall beat them and there'll be no more losses."

"As long as I have you, all I know is profits," Esther answered him.

But the losses did not grow any less. Ezra gave up contracting and started to deal in building plots. Meanwhile Esther gave birth to a second son. The widow Hadjar was still in charge of the household, so that Esther did nothing but look after the babies. Ezra's spirits were not quite so high, and he was hasty and confused in his behavior. Sometimes he would put his finger inside his collar to loosen it, as though that peacock-colored tie of his was on the verge of being transformed into a noose.

Sometimes when Hakham Nehemiah would visit them, Ezra would turn to him and say half-seriously, half-joking, "Perhaps you will tell my fortune, Hakham Nehemiah, that I may know whether my luck has turned against me or not."

"I don't want to hear any fortunes," Esther would

start up and say heatedly, "I don't want to hear them."

"In faith," Ezra would spread out his hand in his distress, "really, I do not know—I was successful all my life, and always on the sunny side of things, but ever since the day I entered this house, I have been in eclipse."

"But this house is yours, *ya-habibi*," said Esther. "What reason have you to complain about it?"

"Ez-ra!" his mother shouted from the kitchen. "There are tools that are unhandy and there are houses that are unlucky. This house has been unlucky ever since it was built."

Esther felt faint and looked inquiringly to her husband. Ezra remained silent. Then she whispered:

"What sort of talk is this, Ezra?" But she gathered her courage together, took the baby from the cradle and picked up her first-born son who was crawling under the table, and presented them to their father. "Isn't this a blessing? Isn't this success? Look!" And she began cuddling both of them at the same time. "Two little stars, may no evil eye harm them, two little stars, may they never fade!"

"With the help of the Lord," responded Hakham Nehemiah.

Ezra ran back to the market, to dash through the crowds, his heart playing a wild tune.

In time Ezra saw that there was nothing for him to hope for from building plots, so he decided to change over and trade in various marbles and mosaic stones; and from that he switched over to precious stones and jewelry. He took out a second mortgage on the house in order to refill his purse and kept buying and selling various articles, but without being able to find profitable merchandise. Finally he went wrong, got himself mixed up in some fraud and was brought to court. He and Esther began spending their time in lawyers' offices, expended large sums on intercessors and bribes; but succeeded in reducing the severity of the law only slightly. Ezra was sent to prison for two years.

The two women were left alone. Their acquaintances and friends kept away from the house. The curtains were again drawn over the windows and the house became dark and gloomy. In her need, Esther began to sell her jewelry and expensive dresses. Simha was dismissed and the widow Hadjar began to do all the heavy work herself. From this point on the old woman dropped the smile from her lips and began to tell her daughter-in-law just what she thought of her. While scrubbing the floors she would sometimes stop all of a sudden, rest on all fours and begin talking:

"Here I am wearing myself out only to save what little good looks you still have; but you are growing ugly, my daughter, growing ugly, and there is nothing that can be done about it. Those extra years that you are older than Ezra are beginning to show —thick and heavy! Oh, the foolish thing he did, poor man! How blind he was—him with the clear eyes! How he ruined himself, not knowing what he was doing!"

Esther stiffened where she sat as though transfixed by an arrow shot from ambush, but immediately calmed herself down. She went up to the mirror, and looked at a yellowing face with sharpening features and black circles of weariness under the eyes. She opened her cosmetics kit, took out some kohl and rouge and casually applied them to her face, saying to herself: She is quite right, she is quite right. She has a mountain of hatred for me in her heart, a whole mountain which I could never move. Father in heaven, give her some of that wonderful medicine of yours, give her some of it!

But the old woman went on slowly scrubbing the floor, and slowly scrubbing at Esther's heart. "The money has vanished like the morning dew," she would cough and say. "The days will fleet like a dream, Ezra will come out still a fresh young fellow, and you will be all worn out." She leaned on her brush, her broad body spreading slack among the puddles of water on the floor, and began wailing: "Ezra my son, what have you come to? Comfort of my life, where they cast you!"

[IX]

At the time Ezra was sent to prison Esther was carrying her third child. On visiting days she used to lock up the house and go with her mother-in-law and children to the grated prison gate. From a distance they could see Ezra in the courtyard, his head shaven and his face gloomy. All that was left of his former good looks was his flashing white teeth. Ezra would grip the grating before him with both hands and thrust his head between the bars, without saying a word. Esther would cup her hands around her mouth and call through the grating:

"Ezra, everything is in order at home."

"And how are you, mother?" Ezra would suddenly rouse himself to ask.

"All right."

"And how are the children?"

"All right."

"And you, Esther, how are you?"

"All right."

"And here I stay and ask myself constantly why I must drink this bitter cup. I don't know, so I think all kinds of things . . ."

"Don't think, don't think, Ezra," Esther would cry out trembling. "Just don't think. Look after your health and don't get angry. The time will pass and you will return home and we shall begin all over again, begin anew."

"Can there be anything new for me under the sun?"

"Why not?" Esther would force herself to smile, pointing with her finger to her swollen belly.

The prisoners standing around laughed. Esther blushed, while her mother-in-law stood there with blinking eyes and quivering lips.

"Rest, Ezra; let your mind rest," Esther called to him at parting.

"I am at ease, I am at ease," he answered her, his head between his arms.

Five months afterward Esther bore her third son. The house began to be emptied of the furniture, and life assumed the character of complete poverty. Esther turned to her brother for help, but he only responded with a few copper coins. She found the burden of living heavy; every day seemed to be a high mountain which had to be climbed.

She climbed many such mountains before Ezra's term was up and he was released. When he returned home Esther breathed freely, as though she had at last arrived at a level plain where walking was easy.

Ezra sat in the empty house, his wife on his right hand and his mother on his left, both of them holding his hands and caressing and embracing him while they passed their fingertips over every wrinkle that had appeared on his forehead, and every line which had been engraved in his face.

"My darling," his wife murmured to him from the right.

"My only darling," his mother murmured to him from the left.

The boys climbed up on his knees and rubbed against his bristling cheek, and Ezra sat smiling, his eyes blank. For hours on end he lay on his bed, his hands folded on his chest and his eyes raised to the ceiling.

"I must make a fortune at one go," he would say cryptically, baring his teeth.

"There is no need to make your fortune. Fortune does not like to be made. You go and find work in an office, and it will not matter. You are strong, thank God, and have good sense. And we shall live quietly, for we have a long life ahead of us. And if we've come down a little, there is no harm done. Our health is the important thing. You will be able to lift your head up once again, Ezra. Why you have not even a single white hair on your head, thank God."

"And where are your bracelets?" asked Ezra without turning his head.

"I can manage without bracelets."

"Where are the silk dresses?"

"If you wish I shall become a washerwoman."

"Ha!" said Ezra.

"I shall go and sell pistachio nuts in the market."

"And what else will you do and sell?"

Esther was silent, and in the silence she gathered together the last of the youth in her heart for a final effort. She brought a smile to her lips and said:

"Have you no pearls in your mouth any longer, Ezra? Come now, come, on your life, and let your tongue wag in the old style. Give me some cheerful word to set my heart ringing with delight."

Ezra gazed at her with smoldering eyes and thought for a moment. " 'Have you no soft plumage any longer?' asked the hawk as it thrust its talons into the bird."

The laughter died in her throat, and her words crumbled. "Am I the hawk, Ezra?"

"In any case I am the plucked bird."

He turned his face to the wall while Esther put her hands in her lap and swayed back and forth.

Ezra began to squeeze every penny she had out of her; he began to take the food from his children's mouths, and to sell the covers and bedding. The women accepted this in silence and never dared to make any complaint. All day he would remain at home, but at night he would slip out, returning only with the dawn. Before long he confided to his wife and mother that he had joined a group of merchants who were going to Turkey on business. But they knew that the company was one of smugglers, with whom he had become acquainted in prison; and that theirs were shady deeds.

Immediately after Ezra left, his mother said to Esther: "Don't talk and don't say anything."

The old woman took to her bed and never left it again, but lay there waiting. A week later they learned that a fight had broken out one night be-

tween the smugglers and the frontier guard, and that
Ezra had vanished without leaving any trace. The
mother died of a broken heart, and Esther was left
alone with her three sons. The creditors brought
pressure upon her to leave the house, and she decided to go back to her father.

She packed up her few remaining things in the
red kerchief that she had inherited from her mother,
and left. When she came to the cellar dwelling, she
opened the door and stopped at the threshold.
Frightened, the children caught at her dress and
stood silent. In the gloom Esther distinguished her
old father, sitting as usual on his mat, leaning over
the sieve before him, building universes of sand and
destroying them.

Esther clasped her hands to her breast and closed
her eyes tight. It seemed to her that no more than a
moment had passed since she had left the cellar.

A PAIR OF identical fig trees had been standing since
time immemorial in that open alley, fig trees whose
dense foliage and scaling barks were unaffected by
the seasons. But in due course one of them was cut
down. Its trunk lay on the ground gradually rotting,
while its bowed twin regularly shed dry young shoots
over it. Between the live fig tree and the dead stood
a tumbledown booth made of four poles covered
with a loose mat. This was the spot that Crazy Rahmiel chose for sleeping. Here he would lie on his
back, wrapped up in rags and tatters, and talk to the
stars during the long night watches. As day grew
bright he would depart, vanishing along with all the
other shades of night, to make way for the little
pushcart of Leah the widow. A heavy little pushcart this was, moving on little wheels, each wheel
inclining at its own angle, each wheel creaking its
own note as it rolled. Leah moved the pushcart by
herself, sometimes pushing it from behind and sometimes dragging it in front. Every little jutting stone
in her way became an obstacle, while hummocks the
height of a little finger seemed like lofty hills. She
groaned, the pushcart creaked, and the Jerusalem
morning blossomed into light that overflowed its
banks.

Once the pushcart was in place under the booth,
Leah would stand still and gasp for breath. Then

41

she would set up a kind of raised footstool to sit on and set out on the board the tired-looking sweets in their wire net, the packages of cigarettes on which lay the dust of many days, the heaps and piles of oranges and grapefruit, and a juice squeezer. Thereafter she would sit silent and dwarfish, a vexed expression on her face and her hands folded idly in her lap. The hours creaked heavily by, seeming to creep like the tiny wheels of her own little pushcart. She would gaze with wondering eyes down the slope of the alley that ran into the main street, patiently awaiting her scrap of luck, as gray as the thin and hollow loaves of the poor. Folk hurried past the entrance of the alley, and one might have supposed that the same people were walking about there, back and forth, all of them searching for something lost that would never again be found.

From time to time a customer would turn up. Sometimes a thick-bearded Kurdi porter would walk over and ask for cigarettes. Leah would energetically wipe the dust from the package, while the Kurdi slowly counted her out the copper coins from his filthy kerchief. Sometimes a pregnant woman going to the Hadassah Hospital would stop to rest, wipe the perspiration from her face and drink a glass of orange juice for the sake of the unborn one. The wrinkles of Leah's face would light up as she smiled at the pregnant woman, carefully pressed the handle so that not a drop of the juice should be left in the fruit, and dropped the peel on the ground at her feet. The cart-wheel sun would grind away on high, and by the time it reached the middle of the heavens the whole world would be burning up with thirst, and people would leave their places one by one and come over to drink orange juice in the shade of the fig tree.

At noon the widow would go home and her place would be taken by her only daughter, who came to take care of the pushcart. Rivkah was a girl of about sixteen, round and soft and gray-eyed, with a tilted nose and a head crowned by a yellow mane. Her faded dress was buttoned up to her chin and her feet were covered with red stockings, which had holes at the bottom so that her ankles could be seen. As soon as she came she would set about to imitate her mother, humping herself a little and giving herself all the appearance of a proper market-woman; but before long she would begin to disregard the pushcart and would turn her eyes to the windows of the houses opposite.

The main street was swept by the sun. Offices and businesses were closed. Clerks and workers went off to take things easy for a couple of hours. But in the alley the day would flow along without either full stop or semicolon; and Rivkah would sit in her booth, silent and lonely like a bride under her canopy.

[11]

A little while before it grew dark three fellows would come and sit down in the shade of the fig tree. First would come Amram the peddler, a keen and lively rhymer with merry eyes and gleaming teeth, who walked about the bus station all day long with a box of sweets of all kinds hanging in front of him. Upon his arrival he would crack a joke with Rivkah; exactly the same one every day.

43

He would come close up, hold his box out to her and cry his wares as usual: "Chocolate fruit, with nuts and milk, sweet as honey, as smooth as silk! Peppermint new, I'd buy if I were you! Buy today when it's cheap, for the stuff doesn't keep!"

And then he would change over, drop the chant and say in his hoarse voice:

"Oh, pardon me, I didn't see that you have exactly the same stuff! So both of us deal in the same goods. Very well, very well, I shan't compete with you, don't be afraid!"

And his smile would shine on her from every hollow in his bony face, while the bristles in the black mop of his hair would stand up like the quills of the porcupine.

After him came young Abraham, reserved and steady, who went from quarter to quarter in accordance with a precise and tested schedule, one shoulder burdened with striped pieces of linen and remnants of cheap stuffs. He would come twirling his yardstick in his hand like the baton of a drum major, slip his goods off his shoulder, choose a piece of bright cloth and say to Rivkah:

"This linen would just suit you, upon my word! The flowers on it are exactly the same as the color of your eyes, a dress like this would suit you to perfection. By my life, you'd look like a princess in town, all the girls would congratulate you and the women will turn green with envy." He would quickly unroll a couple of yards of his stuff and place it against Rivkah's shoulder, dropping it in folds and flounces like a toga, and kiss his fingertips: "Lovely, eh? A dream!"

Rivkah would blush, slip away from him and

cover her mouth with her hand in her shyness.

"In that case," Amram would intervene at this point, "a glass of juice let me take, not in sleep but wide-awake, and I shall drink and be drunk as well, and only buy and never sell!"

He would drink the juice, teetering on his heels with delight, and shake his head as though it had made him drunk.

The third to come would be Pinhas, who sold sun-glasses, razor blades, pencils and similar odds and ends. He was a tall thin lad with a long nose and small eyes, and wore his hat pulled down on his forehead.

"Well?" asked Amram briefly.

"Praise God, praise God," responded Pinhas, putting his hand into his trousers pocket and jingling the coins he had collected.

"In that case," Amram called out to Rivkah, "for Mister Pinhas a glass of juice, for a penny he has no use!"

Pinhas took a sip, smacked his lips and sat down at his ease on the trunk of the fig tree which had been chopped down.

"You astonish me," said Abraham. "Here you go selling razor blades, and yet you yourself have two hairy brushes on your cheeks! What man would ever buy a razor blade from the likes of you?"

"That's the whole point!" responded Amram. "It's a big business secret and you don't know it. When a fellow sees a beard sprouting like this one, he at once becomes afraid and he begins feeling all over his own face to see whether the thorns and thistles are coming up there as well; and he finishes up by buying a blade right off."

"Is that how it is?" chanted Abraham, taking his chin in his cupped palm like a man considering a knotty point in Jewish law. "From which I learn why it is that your face is as bitter as wormwood; just because you go around selling sweet things."

Rivkah would lift her shoulders, laugh into her hand and shift her feet. The three hawkers would turn their eyes on the pink flesh which could be seen gleaming through the holes in the red stockings, above the heels of her worn sandals.

Pinhas would empty his glass and wipe his mouth. "Eh, it puts life into one! And I must have walked a thousand miles on foot today, by God!"

"And why do you have to give your feet such a pounding?" Amram came back at him. "Go and get a job working in somebody else's shop and you'll be done with it. You'll kowtow in front of your boss and you'll get your wages, and you'll be satisfied and so will everybody else."

"No, *ya-habibi*. Me, I am a free man and I want to go on being a free man."

"Oho? Then don't let your mouth make a fuss about your feet."

"That's how the world is made," Abraham would say gravely. "Everybody who is afraid inside, goes and works for others, and everybody who has a brain in his head acts for himself."

"When a man does something, he wants to have something to look forward to," responded Pinhas. "And what can a fellow look forward to in working? When a man works for someone else he gets stuck in one place. But in trade you are a free man, even if you are nothing more than a peddler. Today you'll earn an extra shilling, tomorrow please

46

God another; and so you keep on adding and adding as you go along, and things end up better than they began."

"That was the way all rich folk in town began, all those people with the big shops," said Abraham. "They started out with a peddler's box and finished up with comfort and a round belly, and their shoes always polished and their cheeks bright and shining, and an account in the bank."

"Oho, that road is a little too long!" Amram would laugh. "Why, how about you then, haven't you any time to spare? Have you a short cut to getting rich?"

Pinhas was slowly following along his own train of thought. "You save a little money," said he, "and buy a little house."

"Yes, a house is a good thing to have," Amram would agree with him.

"And particularly," said Abraham casually and without turning his eyes toward Rivkah, "when a man has a good wife who can also turn a penny on her own."

The three peddlers would become silent. Rivkah would fold her arms and begin rubbing her sleeves as though a cold wind had suddenly passed along them. Just then Crazy Rahmiel would come along, hop on his bare feet and come over to the booth. For Rivkah gave him her present every day, and a fine handsome orange it was. Rahmiel scratched at his meager beard, smelled at the orange and murmured, "Ah, ah, it smells like paradise, like paradise. 'The people of Israel shall live!' 'And come with singing unto Zion.' 'Jewish labor!' 'Labor is our life.' "

He slipped the orange inside his filthy shirt. It slipped down under his armpit, and Rahmiel twisted at the tickling sensation and laughed: "Jewish labor, Jewish labor! The people of Israel shall live!" The simpleton twisted, the orange rolled round his body, and the three peddlers burst into hearty laughter. Rahmiel would suddenly stop as though something had come to his mind which he had forgotten. He turned his face to one side, rubbed his feet together and stuck his long nails into the rind of the orange. His eyes were lashless, with dusty lids; and in them gleamed a vast dread. Ever since the light of his mind had failed, he was certain that the world was about to be destroyed.

"In the daytime you can hear nothing," he said. "But at night you can hear. In the daytime this is an orange, but at night it becomes a skull with a brain." He would turn his back on the group and vanish in the alley between the buildings.

If a stranger happened to come along at this evening hour and ask for a glass of orange juice, the three peddlers would immediately move off, sitting down on the trunk of the felled fig tree like three starlings on one bough, crowding together and concealing their stock so that they should not interfere with Rivkah's trade. When the customer had finished his glass and gone his way, Rivkah would put his coin into the rusty jug in the front of the pushcart. The coin would clink and Amram would jump up and announce:

"Boom! another penny to the account. Did you hear?"

"No evil eye, no evil eye!" Pinhas hurriedly spat three times to one side.

"When a coin goes down into the box all her comrades welcome her with tinkling cymbals, but when she leaves the box she departs without a sound. That's how it is!" Amram took two or three mincing steps as though he were walking a tight-rope in his light canvas shoes. 7/- 84/

"Nonsense!" said Pinhas. "I prefer the pound notes, even though they don't make any noise coming or going."

"Go away! You have no ear and no eye. Pound notes are like great aristocrats dressed up in silks and satins, and when they come into the box they don't give crude greetings, but rustle just so, just a little, *ya-habibi,* softly, softly!"

"Just take a look at him," said Abraham, wishing to pull Amram down. "Just look how the chap is licking his lips. By my life, his mouth is dribbling. He's never even had the feel of a pound note between his fingers, and here he is telling all kinds of fairy tales."

Amram stationed himself in front of the company and raised his voice, beating time with his middle finger:

> *Every pound is a thousand mils,*
> *They come marching by so still*
> *And maybe, who knows, maybe,*
> *They are coming here to me!*

"If it were possible to conjure the pounds with songs, you would certainly be a wealthy man by now," said Pinhas.

"I shall be one anyway, God willing," replied Amram. "I've got the feeling I will, and I've got my signs."

"Yet in spite of this you are a miser and a miser you will be, and when you get married, I am sure your wife will perish of starvation. You'll search her teeth for traces of every slice of bread she eats. And if you have any children, you'll be bound to gather them together in the courtyard like a hen's chicks; and you'll scatter a few grains in front of them and you'll say: 'Cheep, cheep, cheep, make the most of this—you'll be satisfied!'"

"When I have a shop," said Abraham gravely, "I shall take the woman who is meant as my match from heaven, and she will remain in the business together with me. I shan't allow her to grow tired or worn out, but she'll stay round with plump limbs and laughing face and delicate hands."

"Of course!" Amram took it up back at him. "So that she would be pinching two or three shillings all the time from out of the money drawer to buy herself all kinds of nonsense, like the womenfolk do nowadays. *I* know!"

"What do you know? You know nothing."

The peddlers began disputing regarding their future wives, apparently talking casually to one another without referring to Rivkah. Yet finally their hearts warmed up and their imagination grew heated. They all began talking at once and interrupting one another, competing in telling jokes and giving vent to pearls of wisdom; while Rivkah sat under the canopy on her elevated seat, moving others, yet herself unmoved; sitting as though all the keys to joy and to delightful hopes had been entrusted to her, all unbeknownst.

When night fell, Rivkah would sometimes light a sooty lamp and hang it above her pushcart. She would wait until her mother came, and then they would push the cart home between them. But more often she would close her business with the dark, jump from her seat, arrange her dress and harness herself to the little cart; and the three peddlers would push along with her, using their hands and their shoulders, cheerfully encouraging her.

"Yallah! Yallah!" their voices would sound while the pushcart creaked and moved along noisily. And the folk in the street would make way for them and watch them as they passed.

[III]

When Joseph Sofiano appeared one day and stopped to drink a glass of orange juice, the three friends became silent all at once and a mood of despondency settled upon them quite unaccountably. Joseph was a young clerk at the post office who spent the whole day behind the bars, with a pencil stuck behind his ear, selling stamps and weighing letters and stamping the envelopes back and front with a big franking postmark.

Rivkah had never seen such a perfect specimen at close quarters. His hair was arranged in regular waves, and his sideburns came down to the middle of his cheek just like the cinema stars. He wore a blue suit even on weekdays and had a gold-checked tie showing in the opening of his jacket, while a handkerchief that was whiter than white gleamed out of the little upper coat pocket. Such young men do not usually quench their thirst in forsaken alleys, but go to cafés where there are soft chairs and where berouged waitresses serve the customers. By chance, however, Joseph had taken a short cut this time on his way back from work, and, feeling thirsty, went up to the pushcart in the alley. At first he paid no attention to the surroundings; but when he sensed the stabbing glances of the three peddlers who sat in a row on the trunk of the felled fig tree, he raised his eyebrows in surprise. He drank, put back the glass and handed over his money with a somewhat pompous casualness, but while doing so glanced at the young girl and saw her gray eyes. Rivkah's face suddenly turned pink, and her constant smile began to entreat in consternation. Suddenly, and like a knife in living flesh, she had felt all the humiliation in the loose mat over her head and the orange peel heaped up at her feet, and all the poverty of the shaky pushcart and the refuse of the life around her.

Joseph nodded in a parting farewell and turned to go, but Rivkah continued to turn his coin between her fingers, and did not drop it into the box.

"Did you see the blessed hand, did you see it?" said Pinhas, without waiting until Joseph was out of earshot.

"How the fellow picked up his coin, eh? You might suppose that his piaster is worth more than anyone else's!"

"Pshsh, like a pasha visiting the country, may God preserve us!"

"And the whole of him I suppose earns a pound and a quarter a month, by my life!"

All at once the three fellows altered their usual style of speech, suspended their internal competition, and began whetting their tongues on the young fellow who had gone away. But Rivkah no longer laughed and no longer covered her mouth with her hand, for all the world as though their witticisms had suddenly lost their point and sting. Absent-mindedly she took the glass from which Joseph had drunk and wiped it with a cloth, her elbows jerking back and forth; she bit her nether lip.

Next day Joseph came again. The peddlers sat huddling together and uncertain in his presence, turned their eyes to the ground and found no more jokes to crack. Joseph leaned against one of the posts of the booth, crossed one leg over the other and deliberately took a long time, taking a single sip and then stopping sipping again and holding his little finger away from the glass in the genteel fashion. Rivkah twisted on her seat not knowing what to do with her eyes. It seemed to her as though there were a dozen pair of eyes in her body, and before she modestly closed one pair another had opened, because they all wished to enjoy the glow of Joseph's splendid face. In her secret heart she was radiant, and astonished at herself. What had a fellow like this seen in her, that he had chosen to come to her pitiful booth in the alley!

Next day the peddlers noticed that Rivkah's mane was no longer tumbling about so merrily, but had been very carefully brought under control with a comb, had been parted, and had been bridled with a ribbon. The peddlers saw this and wondered; they sat wrinkling their foreheads, clearing their throats, and shaking their heads.

Abraham gathered the courage to say, as though to the empty air: "There are lads with bright eyes and a dark heart, and you can never tell where they will lead."

"A girl who keeps her eyes in her head has to be very careful indeed," nodded Pinhas in agreement. "But what can you do if those are just the fellows that the girls run after? It seems that the girls naturally love the dark and the things that are done in the dark."

"Once I saw a girl who had jumped from the roof, from off the fourth floor. It was dreadful. I happened to be passing along the street just then with my goods over my shoulder, and all of a sudden there was something flying through the air, flying and soaring and falling. I was still staring when she lay on the stones in the street, smashed up and pounded to pieces and minced to bits and twisted, with not a single whole limb, simply dead and done for and finished!"

"And in our quarter I knew just such a sort of fellow, you know, a fellow who was all pure and rosy and his soul the most refined olive oil, you might think, with nothing to hide and not knowing enough to add two and two and then he went and did a girl a dirty trick and went off quick to another country, and the poor girl went after him. She had no money and she did not know how to get about, so she strayed into terrible places and nobody knows where she is or what was the end of her."

They went off into terrifying tales which became blacker and blacker, and spun on and on, adding and piling on details. Amram wanted to shake off the mood and to return to happier subjects, so he began singing:

At night as I stood for a while at the gate,
There chanced to pass by me some youth very late . . .

But it was not a cheerful song and did not fit the occasion, so he turned his head aside, tapped his Adam's apple with his finger and became silent.

For several days Joseph came to the booth at the regular time, drank his glass and went his way. When she was alone Rivkah would select the best fruit for him, with thin rind and plenty of juice, and quite a while before the offices closed, her hands would be quivering over the orange-squeezer, and her head turned in spite of herself toward the lane through which Joseph would slowly make his appearance.

He never said anything when he turned up and did not seek any particular intimacy, but preferred to make use of the language of the eyes, a language which is not overburdened, and is composed only of flashes from the pupils and the fluttering of lids and twitching of brows; and those alone were quite sufficient to bring about one transformation after another in Rivkah. On one occasion she noticed that he was looking at her faded dress. The next day she appeared in the booth wearing her Sabbath dress, with short sleeves and a white collar and tassels hanging down on the breast. Joseph glanced casually and saw her red stockings, and the next day she turned up wearing a pair that were flesh-colored, which fitted the calf of her legs perfectly and rounded them out properly. The peddlers would sit with lowering faces, waiting together and watching every movement made by Joseph and Rivkah; wondering without being able to guess whether Joseph had given Rivkah the new stockings as a present, or whether she had gone off and bought them for his sake with her last few pennies. In their confusion each of them began wondering to himself how they could pull that fellow down and subdue him, and get rid of him once for all.

They were still fuming silently at him and boiling over inside, when Joseph suddenly vanished from their sight. They did not know that he had changed his habits and had begun to come and drink his glass of orange juice during the lunch hour, when the alley was empty and Rivkah sat alone in her booth with no watchmen about her. When the peddlers came in the evening they would find Rivkah slack and negligent, with lights flickering in her eyes, no longer turning her head to the lane to listen for Joseph's footsteps. The fellow must have got tired, they decided, and dropped the girl after the fashion of easy-going fellows from time immemorial. They breathed deep, took heart and once again began smiling at Rivkah, and treating her like a convalescent patient. Amram found his voice once more and cheerfully set about rhyming his rhymes, while Pinhas and Abraham again dreamed aloud of a little house and a fitting helpmate; and their tongues wove patterns of scarlet and blue round about Rivkah, marriage talk in hints and indirections.

[IV]

One day when the peddlers arrived at the booth they found that Rivkah was not there. Her place was taken by her mother, the widow Leah, with her kerchief over her head and her gray shawl round her shoulders. Each of them came after his fashion, and each of them asked in alarm: "What's the matter? Where is Rivkah?"

56

And the widow answered three times in her down-cast voice: "She is not feeling well today. It's nothing much, she is a young girl, and it does not mean anything. It will pass, please God, it will pass."

The three of them thrashed about as they stood round the pushcart, tugging their boxes this way and that and staring at one another. "And so you sit here all day long? How is that?"

"And have I a choice? The girl isn't feeling well, so what am I to do? It doesn't matter."

But while she spoke the widow turned her face away from them and did not look them in the eyes, while the lines at the corners of her mouth quivered slightly. How could she go and tell them that Rivkah had been tossing all night long on her bed, and had wept in her lap in the morning and cried: "Mother, mother, tie me up so that I shan't be able to move, because now he wants me to go for a walk with him at night, now he's said to me that I should come by night to our fig tree. Mother, don't let me go, tell me that I mustn't go, because I haven't the strength to refuse. And I don't want to sit in the booth any more, I can't, I don't want to see him. Because if I see him my heart will be as soft as wax."

Such were the words that the girl murmured when the sun rose, just when her mother was preparing to push off her little cart. The widow had stood over her frightened and startled, at a complete loss, and asked: "Should I press out a glass of juice for you to drink before breakfast? It's good, it's very good indeed and very soothing."

The widow had wanted to forget about their business and to stay at home that day, but Rivkah had suddenly become obstinate and cried: "No, no, you go to your stand, but I shan't go." She had sent her mother out of the house, closed the door behind her and become silent.

But these were not things that the widow could tell strangers, so she only shook her head and repeated once again:

"It's only a sickness and it will pass, please God. That's the sort of thing that happens to young girls, and by tomorrow she will already have recovered, with God's aid." And if you like, that was no lie, since in all truth it was a sickness; that inexplicable sickness which burrows at the very foundations of the soul and pulls the sufferer down.

She was still sitting there, brooding over the wormwood in her heart, when Crazy Rahmiel came along, hopping on his bare feet and scratching at his dusty beard. Since he was accustomed to receive his regular orange at this hour, he held out his hand to the pushcart and twiddled his fingers.

"That's all I needed!" cried the widow, shaking the corners of her shawl at him.

"Run along now, and come back another time. Run along!" called the peddlers with angry faces, waving their hands at him.

Rahmiel screwed up his face, blinked hard with his weary and lashless eyelids and threatened them with his finger: "The world is being destroyed, I tell you. You can't hear it by day, but at night you can hear it. You'll see. It will be destroyed. Maybe tonight even. The day has passed, finished. Everything comes out of the night!"

Rahmiel went off, while the peddlers hung about in the shade of the fig tree and waited until the time came for the widow to return home. They wanted to help her and stood beside the pushcart to push it along. But the widow said to them:

"Why are you taking so much trouble for me, my good fellows? Please don't. I shall manage to get home, with God's aid. This isn't the first time, by my faith."

But the peddlers paid no attention, and with compressed lips went off together with her. This time they pushed the cart along separately and negligently, refraining from cries of "Yallah," and folk did not notice them in the street and did not make way for them.

When they came near the house, the widow repeated:

"That's enough, really. Thank you very much. You have gone to a great deal of trouble for an unfortunate woman, and may God bless you."

But once they had come so far, the peddlers asked for permission to enter and see how Rivkah was. The widow opened the door and entered, and all three of them crowded into the doorway in the gloom. In the room a candle was burning in a sandbox, while shadows wavered in the corners among boxes and tins and heaps of all kinds of odds and ends. Rivkah was lying in her clothes on the broad bed, with her face hidden in the pillow. When she heard her mother coming, she jumped up from the bed and asked hoarsely:

"Did he come today?"

"No, he didn't come," said her mother with a downward gesture of her hand. "I didn't see him at all."

"He didn't come?" Rivkah stood confounded, with aimlessly wandering eyes.

Suddenly she noticed the three peddlers who stood together in the doorway without moving. She started up and turned upon them:

"What have you come here for? What have you forgotten here, and what have you come to investigate? Is this a time for visitors? I don't want to see anybody. I want to be alone!"

Her hair was in disorder and without any ribbon. The fingers thrust ahead of her seemed suddenly to have grown long nails, while her chin moved grotesquely up and down.

"It's nothing, nothing," stammered the peddlers, starting back before the girl and the darkness, and closing the door. As they went out they heard Rivkah complaining in a choked voice, with her head in her mother's lap:

"You see, he didn't come. Now he doesn't want to come. Mother, tie me to the bed with cords, for otherwise I shall let the wind carry me away, wherever it will."

"What do I need cords for? I shall hold you hard in my arms. So, so . . ."

The two huddled together like doves, and a faint beam of light threaded through the network of the iron shutter into the gloomy street. For a while the peddlers stood outside, shifting from foot to foot. They could not see one another's eyes, and suddenly they felt like complete strangers with neither speech nor ways in common. Each one settled his burden on his shoulders. They parted from one another with a quick word of farewell, and went their separate ways. Amram alone managed a whistle; and he went on whistling as he walked off.

[v]

The blue night tented over Jerusalem with its pegs in the mountains around the city. Forlorn lamps gazed unblinkingly at the stripped and bare circles of light at their feet. The streets were empty and the stone flags of the pavement stretched along gleaming and attentive, lying in wait for the feet of a solitary walker, catching the echo of his paces and sending it ahead into the distance. In the dark alley two forms sat embracing in the shadow of the fig tree, a boy and a girl.

"Why didn't you come for your orange juice today?" asked the girl.

"Because I wasn't thirsty," said the boy.

"Did you know that I wouldn't come to the pushcart today?"

"I knew that you would come here tonight."

"How did you know?"

They remained silent. The girl waited a moment, and then whispered:

"I can't see in the dark, but I can feel that now you've got the look of a conquering hero."

The boy shifted on his seat.

"Isn't that true? Answer me!" the girl urged him. "Yes."

"Then here you are!" The girl bent toward him, pressed her lips against his and, quivering on his chest, bit long and fiercely.

The boy moaned, started away from her and put his hand to his lips.

"Does it hurt? Does it hurt? Oh, there's blood dripping from your lips, is there? Let me wipe it off. I bit you and I shall cure you."

She took the white handkerchief from his coat pocket and put it to his lips.

"Let me be!"

"Just cry a little, you cry, the way that I cried!"

"And why did you cry?" complained the boy bitterly behind his handkerchief gag. "If you didn't want to, you didn't have to come here!"

"Really?" the girl laughed quietly and covered her mouth with her free hand. "You don't understand anything."

"What don't I understand?"

"I am no longer what I was."

"No? But I haven't even touched you!"

"You donkey!" They were silent for a moment and the girl continued to press the handkerchief against his lips. "Are you still bleeding?"

"Yes. And if you bite again, I shall get up and go away."

"If you are so angry about a little blood, come and bite me back."

"What's this, have we come here to shed blood?"

"I don't know. I don't know what you're supposed to do to make things right. Do you know?"

The boy did not have time to answer, for just then Crazy Rahmiel came into the alley, passed through the passageways like a shadow and approached his sleeping-corner between the fig trees. For a moment he stood silent, then he raised his eyes to the stars and began to pour out his heart to them. The two

62

figures started from their place and vanished, and in the confusion the girl let the handkerchief drop.

Rahmiel paid no attention to those who fled, but opened his nostrils wide and drew deep into his lungs the sweetish smell of the rotting orange peels under the booth.

"The scent of paradise, the scent of paradise," he murmured to himself.

He sat on the trunk of the felled fig tree and began to arrange himself lengthways upon it, but saw the white handkerchief on the ground. He bent over, picked it up by a corner and ran with it to the lamp at the corner of the street. He opened the handkerchief by the light of the lamp, gazed at it, saw the bloodstains, screwed up his face and began shouting:

"Blood! Blood! The world is going to be destroyed! It's really beginning! Their hearts' blood is flowing and they don't know it! That's the finish, the sand in the hourglass has run out and there is no hope for mercy! I'm the only one who can see it! I'm the only one! They're asleep and their eyes are closed, and I am the only one who is awake with wide-open eyes!"

For a long while he danced in front of the lamp, capering in the chilly air, waving the stained handkerchief like a flag, and wondering at the world for still standing amid the roars of destruction and not collapsing.

I AM TAKING to the road today, going on a hike along the bypaths of the Land. You leave En Hatzor the way I do, and find that you're full of the comfortable feel of a settlement that has been standing on one spot these forty years. You set your feet on the uneven roadway and move right along, just looking straight ahead, letting your thoughts run on. Absent-mindedly, you reach Bet Sokho, where the small kvutzah is, without having had the time to have got into the right mood for the charm of a place that is almost four years old. So it is nice of Providence to have managed to prepare a hidden path for you, one that winds around the shoulder of the mountain. It drags out the time, and gives you that extra walking distance you need. You start slowly along the path, and every time you lift your eyes you have a good chance of seeing what's coming and what you've left behind. Behind you lie the shuttered houses of a settlement, with red-tiled roofs that are shaded by thick, shaggy, untended trees; ahead of you are the cubes of snow-white buildings that belong to the kvutzah, open to the heat of the sun and the rage of the winds.

Still, you finally reach a place where the path turns, a spot that's just four by four, where a bulge in the mountain looms over you. Once you get that far, both the settlement and the kvutzah vanish out of sight. All of a sudden you find yourself far from civilization, alone with yourself and your Creator. Here is a tumbledown booth, still standing from the bygone days of the watchman. It is full of mounds of earth and bundles of dry branches. There's a door made of tin plates, hanging by the fragment of a hinge, and creaking very quietly when the wind comes its way. You lean your back against the door and look down the mountain side, seeing crannies in the rocks and flat slabs that seem to be biting into one another. Silence spirals up to mingle with the rays of the sun. The silence covers everything in wrappings of undulant heat until all seems to tremble into sheer oblivion. Three thin cypresses are caught in the middle of the stony clods, like wayfarers who have lost their way and huddle together, staring at the horizon. Piled-up clouds float in the sky, trailing their shadows behind them on the earth, where they drag along and hang over one mound after another. Wherever their shadows fall, they cloud over the gleaming smooth rocks round about. You might imagine that some huge wing were covering the face of the earth for a little while.

It was a whole year and a quarter I spent at En Hatzor, working two or three days a week, but now the colony gets along quite nicely without me. The old houses are signaling me to that effect from their little windows. The houses are just like the farmers who won them: morose, tight-lipped, and wrinkled with hardships. The work came to an end, but I spent another two months or so drifting about the streets all day long and staring into the courtyards, hanging about the hut of the employment office or lying on my mattress, just idling.

Well, there was idleness just around the corner,

encroaching like the rust and afflicting the spirit with a lean consumption that verged on the twilight of death. At the end of the second month it became clear to me that I must get up and go away to some other place.

So I put the few things I have in my knapsack, together with half a loaf of bread and a couple of tomatoes; and I look strange and unrecognizable to my little room.

My lodging had been in the teachers' hut, and during rainy weather narrow runnels of water had made their way between the cracks, while during the sunny season I was scorched by skewers of sunbeams. The teacher had aged and his shoulders were slack, but his glasses still flickered with the fitful gleam of the scholar. He has no children and he takes pleasure in wordplay.

I dropped in to say goodbye and he wrinkled his brow and thought, trying to think of a few cheering words to say to me. His glasses darkened for a moment, but when the flickers of light returned he said: "You are going away? Naturally, for how can a Jewish lad remain in one place?"

He takes his glasses off his nose and wipes and polishes them, laughing and twitching with his wizened body. I leave him, and go across to the office exchange to say goodbye to the lads. But the only people I find at the office are the secretary and Moshe Adir. "Where to?" asks the secretary, looking up. He wears the embroidered blouse of the old-timer, but his knickers are short and the legs sprouting out of them are long and very thin. A fine speaker he is, and even took part in the debate at the last country-wide conference.

"I want to look for work somewhere else," say I

to him. My voice is nervous and has a sort of defensive tone which was not at all intended.

The secretary screws his mouth and whistles and puts his pencil down, and promptly starts in just like an old hand: "And here I was thinking that we were already attached to the spot like leeches. . . . That we would not be blown away by any breeze that happens to come along. . . . Of course the situation is bad, but we cannot afford to let any of the positions slip away. . . ."

"Yes, yes, that's it," Moshe Adir interrupts him, his eyes dull and his face sullen. He twists his lips and turns to me: "Off to town, eh? To get a taste of things, eh?"

At this point it occurs to me that I have not yet decided how far away I want to roam, and I stammer irrelevantly:

"It's two full months that I haven't known what it is to do a stroke of work here."

"Only two months?" asks Adir, screwing up one eye and swinging his bare feet back and forth. I used to work in town with Adir, and in those days he used to jabber a lot about world revolution. In those times he used to screw up one eye too, and it was for his sake Ada left the kvutzah, the same kvutzah that afterward settled at Bet Sokho. Gray eyes has Ada, and a couple of freckles on the bridge of the nose; and her upper lip turns upward slightly when she smiles. Her little girl has a high forehead like Adir's. For a long time Ada used to work very hard at a co-operative laundry, and lived in a tent with Adir on the outskirts of the town. Adir has a mop of grayish hair which shows no sign of age, and he left Ada all of a sudden and cleared off to Galilee.

Now he is one of the idlers round this place. No, I do not have Ada in mind any longer, but just the same I can't find anything very cordial to say to Moshe Adir for goodbye.

I leave the office exchange and pass the house of the farmer for whom I last worked. The farmer is busy in his courtyard, and when he sees me with my knapsack on my back he hurriedly turns his head away and begins fumbling with the harness of his mules. I want to go and start talking to him, but say to myself: A strong impulsion once drove these folk to this desolate spot. Now that wind has gone its way, and has left nothing there except vestiges of human beings, and fields once watered now smitten with drought.

I drag my feet as I walk between the rows of houses, looking in every direction and casting up my accounts as I go along. Here is where I worked for eighteen days, and here I invested all of twenty-three. The weeks add up, and my account is in order, to the total of a year and a quarter. There is only one day missing. I try my best for a while to remember how I spent it, but I can't recall. And all the time my feet stay stuck to one spot, as though to hint, "We are not going to budge until that account has been properly balanced."

I make the rounds of every corner of my memory, and conduct a strict self-examination, until I discover the day curled up in a dark nook. It was the day when I heard that Ada had come to Bet Sokho with her little girl on a visit to her old kvutzah. I let a day's work go hang, put on a white shirt and set out for Bet Sokho. But when I reached the gate, it struck me that Ada must really have come to Bet

Sokho to meet Adir there. So I turned on my heel, and went back where I came from.

After having carried out this census of my time, I feel better. The road flows straight ahead till you come to Bet Sokho; it shimmers in front of my eyes. I once went for a walk with Ada on such a road, in one of the settlements of Judea. That was her third year in the Land. And Ada had said at that time, "Do you know—I am afraid of the passing days."

I had laughed at that time, with rather foolish arrogance, and said, "But why should you be afraid? We still have enough and to spare in our knapsack!"

She looked down at the ground, and asked me, "Is that why you've remained all alone until now?"

"I don't know," I answered. "Maybe I have been waiting for you all these years."

She didn't say a word, but her fingers began busying themselves with her hair, undoing the braids and plaiting them over and over again. Then she began to sing in a low voice:

> *Wordlessly, I cover my face*
> *In the delight of setting days.*

My feet leave the road and go round the houses of En Hatzor of their own accord, leading me to the hidden path. I stroll along at my ease. It is one o'clock in the afternoon. My idea is to reach Bet Sokho just as night is falling. The comrades will be returning from their day's work around that time. They will pass me and wonder what that fellow is doing on a hike on a day that is neither a Sabbath nor a holiday. They will hurry over to the showers, while I hang around between the cowshed and the poultry run, until the fellow in charge of the yard comes my way. I shall tell him almost faintly that I want to spend the night there and go off to the next colony with the milk cart in the morning. The fellow will look at me and think of something else. He'll wrinkle his forehead, like someone trying to resume an interrupted conversation, and finally end up with the established formula, "You can sleep in the bed of the chap who's going on guard."

I have been in the kvutzah a number of times now, to listen to itinerant lecturers, or just for a Sabbath stroll. But I have no acquaintance or close friend there. I know all about their farm. I am quite aware of the fact that their winter crops have done well this year. They are still debating whether to drop peas from the list of rotating seeds, and they are about to extend the area under cultivation with barley and maize. They have planted two rows of olive trees, and expanded the wood patch on the hill slope.

But when I sit down at their table in the dining hall, I am sure to fidget in my seat and twiddle my fingers. The girl whose turn it is to serve will hand me a bowl of soup, and I'll suddenly feel a large lump in my throat, and, quite unnecessarily, will begin stirring the soup. In just the same way I'll stir about in my mind trying to find something to talk about with my neighbor. I know for certain that my neighbor is bound to be one of the youngsters who have come directly from the ship's deck to the kvutzah yard, without having passed through any of the intermediary stations. He'll be calm and secure, like a son who has returned to the bosom of his family, and I shall start to stammer odds and ends about the worker's life in a settlement. My neighbor will listen, all afire, and wonder will start up in his eyes, like a child listening to a fairy tale about sufferings and adventures of the faraway.

After that the night will come, and the comrades will scatter in different directions. I shall stroll about alone, bored and at a loss, and listen to the laughter coming out of their rooms.

And then the silence will come, and I shall have to grope through pitch darkness to find the room of the chap who is on guard. Weary, feeling all muzzy, I shall drop down on his bed, without any idea of who that could be snoring on the other side of the room. I shall cover myself with a rough blanket, and inhale the smell of an unknown body from the sheets; and I shall not be able to sleep. With morning, the owner of the bed will come in, shake me by the shoulders to get me up, and hoarsely growl his annoyance. I shall start up, dress quickly, rinse my face with cold water, and go out to gulp down a glass of something hot. And, again, I shall have no one to take leave of; the milk cart will start slowly, while I ride clattering among the cans, dragging my fate behind me.

It is still broad daylight and there is not much farther to go. I slow down in response to the windings of the narrow trail, until I reach the tumbledown booth. I am not in the least weary, but because I have nothing to do I go into the booth and stretch out on the heaps of earth and dry twigs. The chinks in the roof are patched with strips of pure blue. I am offered an odd piece of horizon through the crack of door lying on its side; and in my wallet there are half a loaf of bread and two tomatoes. That is the sum total of ten years' work. Road-making and buildings, camels and orange groves, grain-growing and watching by night, all of them flavored with any number of months of unemployment and sickness. Ten years all in all, and the balance to my credit is half a loaf and two tomatoes.

The bread has dried and spotted in the heat, while the tomatoes have warmed up in my knapsack and are going moldy. From the entrance of the tumbledown booth the day moves toward its conclusion; and the patches of green in the hills gradually grow black. Once I sat with Ada telling her all about my childhood in my grandmother's house. Ada had seemed not to pay attention to anything but peeling oranges and arranging the pieces one next to the other on a plate. She turned her eyes to me and said: "I want to look for a piece of life for myself that will not have the flavor of grandmother's house."

The freckles quivered on her nose and her upper lip lifted. . . .

There is still a trace of fragrance in the dry twigs in the booth. I wrap myself in the silence and close my eyes. Where are the ten years I planted here, in the Land? It might be worth while for me to take my knapsack and make the rounds of the settlements all over the country, putting on a small exhibition —a chunk of bread and two tomatoes, and the charred remains of ten years of a man's life. Not that I blame the Land or people. Let anybody who wants to, come and see for himself, and take it to heart. And how about beginning today? Supposing I were to get up in the dining hall at Bet Sokho, when we all sit down to eat, and take out my bread and tomatoes, and lifting up my hands, wave them in the air, saying with a laugh: "Just look at this!"

Then those youngsters would turn to me with frightened eyes, and be astounded at this chap talking to them about bread and tomatoes instead of about a transformation of values and the problems of mixed farming. No, I am not short of things to think of. My thoughts come crawling along of their own accord. Maybe they are what's making me stir, or maybe there is something rustling among the dry twigs.

I open my eyes, and see the head of a snake in the crack of the door, for all the world as though my thoughts have taken on a sensible form. The snake twists and winds over the stones until he gets the greater part of his body into the booth. My heart melts, I break out in a cold sweat, and my mind almost clouds over.

Through my memory flashed the morning when I was hired to cut up a pile of old railroad ties. The man who gave out the work was an old man from the German colony, and the split ties were sold in advance to Ada's co-operative laundry. I didn't see Ada at the time, but her little girl was rolling in the sand nearby. I was moving some of the ties, when a snake came out and started toward the playing baby. Startled, I stood frozen to the spot; but the old Gentile who was standing next to me jumped fast, grabbed the snake near the neck, laid it on a block and chopped its head off with an ax.

Afterward, when I told Adir what had happened, he twisted his lip, screwed up an eye, and said: "A fellow like you is never capable of taking a snake by the neck."

74

The snake in the booth rises a little and gazes into my terrified eyes. He shakes his head back and forth as though he had been watching for and had found his companion-thoughts in my eyes.

"Having a heart-to-heart talk with yourself?" say the moving lips of the snake. "One thing is absolutely certain: A man like you will never jump out and grab me by the neck and swing an ax against me." It seems to me that in a moment he'll screw up one of his eyes and flickering gleams of laughter will be sunk in the wrinkles of the other. "Oh no, it wouldn't suit you to do anything of the sort. You and your kind can't do anything to the snakes of the world. You've only one weapon, and that's the flute. Just you make sure always to have a flute in your belt. Then, whenever you see a snake nearby, you can start fluting. True, the snake will never be got rid of that way, but his head will sway like a dancer and you'll have saved yourself for the time being."

I kneel on all fours feeling faint, my throat as dry as a crock. I have the answer in my heart. I could tell him about ten years of my life, during which I played on my flute and made my snakes dance whenever they raised their heads. But the fellow I'm talking with doesn't want to listen. He opens his mouth, flickers his tongue at me, and goes back where he came from.

I jump to my feet and open the door of the booth. The afterglow of the sun is parting from the sky, and shadows extend into the crannies of the hills. The night arrives from a far journey. The tops of three solitary cypresses quiver, and recite a blessing over the first star shining in the sky. I carry my knapsack on my shoulder, and carry on an argument with myself; now what does that belly-crawler think? Now he'll see whether I shan't grasp a snake by its neck, or do what I was thinking of doing at Bet Sokho!

My knees are still shaking from the frightening experience, but I take long, vigorous strides, with one hand swinging free. I concentrate, forbidding my eyes to turn to the fields of color that spread richly in the west. There's a light wind touching my neck, but I don't answer it. As I face the horizon, the day is still bright and calm and the sunset tidings have not yet caught up with it. By the time I reached Bet Sokho it was dark everywhere. The noise of voices and the clatter of spoons and plates rise from the dining hall. Supper is almost over, and I hesitate to go in. I go over to the cistern, and stand there, waiting for the fellow in charge of the yard. The empty pitchers, washed for the early morning milking, stand gleaming at me. The light pours calmly through the open windows, and on the horizon the mountains get their teeth in the sky, and pluck garlands of light for their darkened heads. The vast spaces of night had been added to the territory of the small land. Grasshoppers are already shrilling on every side, and the hour, passing away, banks the remnants of the coals that darken the heart.

Suddenly, I begin to be painfully hungry. I sit down on the trough under the cistern, loosen my knapsack, take out my bread and tomatoes and begin furtively chewing. If anybody were to pass by now, I'd squint with one eye and pretend that all I am interested in is the stars up on high. They waver, and dot the letters in the scroll of the sky; the sickle of the quarter moon tramples on the deep blue. A chill solitude flows in on me in a sevenfold stream but a sharpened fire is in me, that will not, relaxing, evaporate. I dip my hand in the lukewarm water in the trough, take it out and wet my face.

The door of the house opens, and the members of the kvutzah come out and go their separate ways. I stand up and grope about in search of the fellow in charge of the yard, and without noticing it I find that I've reached the ridge on the slope of the mountain. The young trees seem to have lined up on either side if that were possible, and to have put on robes of darkness, and as a result seem to the eye to be closer together and larger than they really are. A rustle of conversation trickles from the other end, and I listen against my will.

In the darkness a girl begins to sing a song of long ago:

Wordlessly I cover my face . . .

And I spread my legs, plant them firmly on the ground and send my voice ringing through the empty air:

In the delight of setting days . . .

The unseen girl is silent for a moment; then she goes on with the tune:

In the delight of setting day-ays . . .

For a brief moment we stand calling to one another, in invisible song. My face is still wet, and so are my eyes. Probably with the lukewarm water from the trough.

THOSE ARE strange trees towering over my fence. They come up fast and their foliage spreads far and wide, but the roots do not really strike deep into the soil. It seems as though there is something lacking in their natural instincts, so that they aren't quite what trees ought to be. I only need to scratch a little around the base of their trunks to lay bare tangles of bulbous cords and fibers gripping clods of earth. In a couple of days I shall be packing up and leaving this place, and I shall never know what happens to these trees when the storms and the tempests come. But anyway, they are good for spreading out a mat under during the sunny hours, and it's good to lie with your eyes closed. The foliage weakens the sun's rays and all kinds of thoughts go drifting across your mind. Some of them pass as they come, while others go into concealment to return in dreams at night.

I may as well confess that my spare time is much too plentiful, and that's a bad thing. In view of my lame leg the only job I could get was being a watchman in a large warehouse for building materials. I don't know why the warehouse had to be so far from the town or, for that matter, why the owners decided to hire a cripple to watch it. Maybe what attracted them was the very low wages I asked, or maybe they came to the conclusion that a cripple is not so likely to get frightened easily. Whatever their reason may have been, this was my post and my home. Trucks came every day either to take merchandise out of the warehouse or to stock up. At intervals the warehouse owners would turn up, go to my room and check. Mine is a small room, and most of it is occupied by an iron bedstead, although I have never yet slept the whole night through in it since coming here. Two or three times a night I would get up, and go out to make the rounds. I would carefully pick my way among the piles, planks and pipe in the yard, look all around and prick up my ears. Sometimes I would leave the yard and shuffle along the lonely path. Afterward I'd turn about and take a look at the big warehouse from the distance. The light coming out of the window of my room always looked orphaned and lonely, like a memorial candle.

A little distance from the warehouse and in full view lies the kvutzah of Tel Hayyim. Though only five years old, the kvutzah is girdled by an avenue of trees, and behind are green squares of garden and field. Lying on my mat among the trees I can watch all that is going on in the Tel Hayyim courtyard. Children hop about in the grass, and puppies romp with them. A horse-drawn wagon returns from the fields, driven by a chap standing upright. The blade of a plough flashes from under a sack and gleams in the sun. A cow takes her time at the trough, and the saliva drips from her mouth to the ground.

The gong in the kvutzah used to cut across my day as well as theirs, and when it sounded at noon I would get up and prepare my meal. From time to time I would go across to Tel Hayyim to get some food or to borrow a book. Sometimes I would drop in there for a little while in the evening to listen to a lecture. When I left in the dark I would meet their watchman, walking around with his rifle on his shoulder. We would both pause a moment and have a brief conversation.

"Seems to me it's hard to walk on this path," I say. "The ground is damp and the earth sticks to your boots."

"Indeed?" says the chap in surprise, shifting his feet about to see whether I am right.

We smoke a couple of cigarettes and blow the smoke directly in front of our faces. The horizon turns deep blue, and the headlights of passing cars flash along the distant highway.

"Plenty of traffic on the road tonight," says the fellow.

"Yes," say I, "folk must be going off to town to have a good time."

"No," says the fellow, "it's only Arabs coming back from a wedding."

Silently we look at our surroundings. Maybe the lights of the cars on the highway are real life, while we humans are on the outside of it all. Or maybe we are the fixed and permanent stuff of the world, while those lights are the stuff that dreams are made of. The silence is everywhere, and we two night watchmen look for no subject about which to exchange our words. For us it is clear that this small country has been blessed with a little too much sky, for the eye and heart to contain. The earth stretches tight from one end of the horizon to the other, laboriously supporting that huge blue dome, and deep in the earth the grasshoppers drone longingly. A breeze rustles among the reeds, and a silent bat swoops through the empty air like a fragment of the black and blind things of the world.

We part. Each of us goes his way. In a little while the lights will go out in the kvutzah, and after that the only light left burning in all the region will be the one in my window. For quite a while longer young couples will be walking along the rows of half-grown trees, singing their songs of bygone days. A blouse will gleam white in the distance, a girl will burst out laughing from the secret depths of her breast, and a voice will call long and loud out of the darkness:

"Shmue-e-e-el, have you rinsed the pitchers?"

Little by little the night is going to cut short the last gasps of the day and reduce the world to silence. To tell the truth, the daytime is when I exist, but I live at night. During the daytime I know for a certainty that the earth revolves on its axis and goes around its sun, and I know for an absolute certainty that the blue skies are nothing but an illusion. But at night it seems to me as though I believe in God. I sit on a heap of pipes in the yard, and pick out all the different smells around me: the smells of planks and boards in the warehouse, the smell of manure and fallow land, the smells of trees and grasses, and all those other odors that pass through this long passageway known as life-on-earth. All of a sudden the thought occurs to me: Maybe, after all, there is really somebody in the big hall yonder at the end of the passageway?

If that watchman chap were to come over here now I might talk the idea over a bit with him. This is the right time to talk about the mysteries of the soul, for whoever you may be talking to can't look you in the eye and see how shamefaced you are. But the watchman over at the kvutzah never comes this way, since I am outside his bounds. I lift my eyes up, but the night around me is high and lofty and will talk to me of nothing but stars and death.

When I start thinking about death, all the trifles of daily life suddenly come to mind. I remember that one of the legs of my bed is shaky, that I forgot to buy eggs at the kvutzah, that I forgot to fill my lamp with kerosene and it may go out at the end of the first watch. Impatiently I get up and walk about until the darkness comes back and covers me.

I am convinced that a man on the verge of death hears wings beating over his head, just like that poet who used to hear the rustle of wings whenever a fresh poem began taking shape within him. When the trouble with my leg first began, a heavy cloud settled over my heart and I wanted to die. But every man finds his own rainbow in his own cloud. I found all kinds of peculiar pretexts to go on living. I conjured up the face of my old mother in her little town far away in the Diaspora. I convinced myself by means of decisive arguments that our country can do without none of its inhabitants, not even its cripples. I worked myself up into a fever of curiosity to know what was coming next and what the future had in store for me.

When I woke up in the hospital after my anesthetic, I heard Rachel crying and saying to the doctor:

"Oh, we don't know how to value the little life we've been granted!"

From the moment I opened my eyes Rachel was there looking after me. She never took off her white coat and never left me day and night. When I left the hospital, she came to my room every evening as usual to prepare tea and cook something for me to eat. I was ashamed because of that lame leg of mine, and when she came I would just sit in a chair and never budge.

She would walk about, chatting of this and that, clearing one corner and fixing up another; but finally she would get tired of all that, and her face would fall all at once. Then the broom would slip from her hands and she would slump to the sofa, cross her hands in back of her head and begin to sing. One song would follow another and the tunes would merge. Tunes with words and tunes without words, folk songs and fragments of opera in Hebrew, in Yiddish, and in other languages. She would sing without moving and I would listen without moving.

One evening I gathered strength and said to her, as a kind of hint:

"You know, my stride has grown shorter and I can't walk fast any more. I am afraid I shall not be able to keep up with you."

"Nonsense," says she, "I am not in the least anxious to walk fast."

When she spoke, she did not turn her head to me or smile but raised her eyes to the ceiling. I saw a little vein pulsing at her temple, and I saw that one of her legs was swinging carelessly in front of the sofa. A curl had dropped over one eye, but she did not blow it away.

"Come and kiss me," she said in a hoarse voice. "It is so long since you've kissed me."

I was seized with dread. I turned my head to the window. How could I go over for a kiss with this lame

84

leg, how could I cross that vast distance of three and a half paces with my stick?

I sat motionless, my tongue dry in my mouth.

"Well then, I shall come across to you," said she with a pretense of daring. She jumped off the sofa and began to arrange her hair and her dress, as though she were really preparing for a distant journey.

But she did not set out on the distant journey. She suddenly remembered that she had to go and find out something about her next day's work.

I don't know, maybe she really had to go, the way she said she did, she did not have a steady job at that time. Yet I was certain that she would never come back to me any more; nevertheless, I did not move a finger to stop her. I remained where I was, and she left the house. In due course, she found work in Jerusalem and went to live there. I came to accept things as they were, and once that happened I began limping about as I pleased. Something within me settled down and I stopped knocking at closed doors. I suppose my smile must have grown slightly mocking, and I no longer pretended that my walking stick was just an ornament. But my worst trouble was that I had far too much free time.

I used to lie lazily on my mat, overtowered by strange trees. Through the latticework of the fence I could see Tel Hayyim and all that was going on there. White houses and a high water tower, sown flower beds and a whirling water-sprayer, boards of chicken roost, and linen drying in the sun. A new building going up, its beams projecting in every direction. Cropped plants and tender seedlings were standing as though they were ashamed.

I would ask myself: Who will be the first to die here? How can a building of life go up without a graveyard monument behind it? My first estimate is that something will doubtless happen to one of the small children there. The kvutzah consists chiefly of young couples, and there are a lot of small children who can always be expected to fall sick with things like diphtheria and scarlet fever and measles and all kinds of stomach poisoning. To be sure, the death of a child does not really apply, for it's not of the proper proportions. When a young plant withers and dries up, there isn't enough in it to enrich the soil. But that does not apply to a tree with a large trunk and lofty bole and many roots. In any case, even the children at Tel Hayyim are healthy and bright, and kick about in their playpens with soft little legs while their faces grow sunburnt. If I sometimes hear a baby crying in the distance at night, I can be certain that it is only a passing sickness and nothing really serious.

So I change my mind and decide that doubtless something will happen to one of the grownups yonder. There are two or three old workers, chaps who are bald and bowed already, and have wrinkled faces. There are two or three fellows who suffer intestinally, and writhe with cramps every now and then. But I made inquiries and found that they are all sent off to town at regular intervals, spend some time taking their ease in hospitals and convalescent homes and come back partly rejuvenated. They and their like are just the people who know how to stave off the end and live to a ripe old age. Why, even the fellow whose mare kicked him is fit again after a few weeks. He is weak, to be sure, and one shoulder is higher than the other, and he can only tackle light work. Yet in spite of everything, he is still lively enough to whistle and laugh and dance a hora with the next man at a pinch.

Whenever I went over to the kvutzah, I would take a good look at the comrades whom I met in the yard. I couldn't get rid of that thought knocking at my heart. In spite of myself, I had to keep my eyes down for fear someone should notice me and spot what I am thinking about them. It seems to me that that little untended patch next to the young wood the kvutzah planted must have been marked off as a graveyard. But for the time being it stands unfenced. Children play games and cats sun themselves there.

Once while crossing the courtyard I pretended ignorance, shaded my eyes with my hands and asked a fellow who was just passing:

"That plot over there—why are you leaving it fallow?"

The chap looked in that direction and mumbled a couple of words:

"Looks as though it hasn't been decided . . . some plan or other . . . "

He turned away and hurried off to work.

Do the comrades think about it sometimes, or do they purposely disregard the whole business? The yearnings of the nation, historic connection, the Land of the Fathers where the prophets trod—all this is words and no more. A grave is needed here, a white stone memorial flaunting a big "HERE LIES," surrounded by thorns and briars and silence, gleaming amidst the tree trunks as a dumb witness of roots and the continuity of existence.

I lay alone on my mat and the days passed me by. Nothing new happened to me, apart from a tiny garden of four by four which I cleared between my trees and planted with flowers. I also grew a climbing vine which twined around my fence, adding an air of charm to the spot. Nor did anything new happen over at the kvutzah, except that three of the comrades fetched their parents over from the Diaspora. From my hiding place, I could watch the three old men walking about together in the courtyard as though at a loss for what to do, their long black *kapotes* bobbing slowly in the distance.

In due time I went over to the kvutzah yard one afternoon. I found the old men sitting next to one another, in the shade of the narrow terrace in front of the dining hall. The yard was empty. The three old men leaned on their sticks as though bowing over the last remains of their vitality, and stared straight ahead. At my arrival they turned their heads in my direction and gazed at me with dull eyes.

I stood still in front of them and said loudly, "*Shalom!*"

"*Shalom*," they answered in unison, chewing the Hebrew word over in their mouths, their long beards trembling a trifle. They seemed to be hesitant, as though uncertain whether I belonged to the kvutzah.

"I live over there, I do," I said to put them at ease, pointing to the distant warehouse. "I have only come here to greet three Jews who have come up to the Holy Land."

"Yes, yes," murmured all three of them, blinking.

After a brief silence one of them stirred and asked in businesslike fashion:

"And what are you up to in that building over yonder?"

"I am a watchman."

"Aha!" said all three of them, cheered by this unexpected diversion.

"Well, and how does this place strike you?"

"Thank God, there is everything here," answered one of them.

"Thank God, thank God," the two others responded after him.

"Yes, this is a fine settlement," said I as well. "There is everything here, almost everything."

They became silent, as though I had insulted them by saying something forbidding. I went away leaving them sitting in a row, their skullcaps on their heads and their shirtsleeves gleaming white.

Again the days passed and nothing happened at Tel Hayyim. Morning after morning I could see the old men in the distance coming out into the yard after their prayers on their way to the dining hall to drink something hot. After that they would go back to read a book or study a chapter in the Mishnah. At noon all three of them would pass through, holding dishes in which to carry from the kitchen ritually prepared food which they would eat in their rooms. After that they would lie down to rest and take a nap. In the late afternoon they would go out again and slowly take a walk round about the courtyard, gravely inspecting their surroundings, lifting a piece of a utensil or a rusty tin can from the ground, straightening out a branch that had become twisted in one of the trees, or clasping their hands behind them and going for a little stroll beyond the confines of the yard.

At night I would think of other things. I would give myself over to thoughts of my own, while the moon above hovered over me.

From the outside I look at the light in my window and I say to myself: If only God were to show by a sign, the faintest sign, that he is present in the world! Then the world would become more wide and spacious and be rejuvenated all over again, like an old tree when the breezes of spring pass through its boughs. Oh, only a faint sign, for without it you can see nothing these our days, you can see not a whisper of the existence of God, you can see nothing but the traces of footprints along a path where nobody passes any longer.

My thoughts go off on their own tack, and finally I cannot make head or tail of them myself. My night, so to say, stares at my day without being able to understand it. The night goes along ahead of me, so to say, while I limp halting after it. My shadow drags unwillingly after me, as though it would prefer to be the shadow of somebody else. If I were sure that the watchman over at the kvutzah was sick of being alone, I would go over and have a chat with him.

One morning while I was weeding my little plot, a cart left the kvutzah yard with two lads in it.

Where can they be off to at this hour? I wonder to myself. My wonder grows as the cart turns into my own courtyard. "Oho," says I to them. "My house has never been so honored. Two comrades at one and the same time!"

They smile faintly and tie the reins to the post of the cart. They need wood. They have come over to buy a few boards and planks.

"What's the matter? Do you propose to run up a couple of new mansions?"

No, they only have to fix up a terrace in the last house in the kvutzah. It is a little building that stands apart from the rest, and a new tenant is coming to live there.

I put down my hoe and wipe the sweat from my brow. "A new tenant?"

Yes, that fellow whose name everybody knows, who has spent his whole life redeeming the Land for Israel. Now that he has grown old and gray and weary he wishes to live quietly and spend his last days in a new settlement. He is all alone, his wife died long ago and he has no children; and now he wants to live in the company of young folk.

"That's fine, fine," says I to the lads, spinning on my sound leg with real delight. "It's really fine that he should have hit on your place of all places."

I select excellent planks for them and perfect boards, and the craftsmen over at Tel Hayyim went hard to work. Scarcely had they finished their job when a truck arrived bringing all kinds of fine furniture, and cases and boxes. Finally a handsome gleaming motor car arrived as well, with the honored new resident. The new terrace which the lads made for him is out of my sight, since it stands behind the house and looks out over the fields and the distant mountains. From my yard I cannot see what is going on there, but I imagine that the old man is doubtless lying in his easy chair, fetching out memories and fragments of memories.

After three days have passed I see him crossing the yard for the first time. He is tall and lean, with long gray hair falling down to his shoulders, and his knees tremble badly. Behind him walks a nurse sent to look after him and prepare his special diet, while a furry black dog romps beside him. Indeed this is a magnificent ruin, the ruin of a great man who has achieved much and has now come to the end of his earthly path. If it were not for the stick in my hand, I too might put my finger in my mouth like those children yonder in the kvutzah yard, and casually look at him with wonder as he passes in front of me. His skin is very shriveled and his hands tremble, his lower lip hangs loose, and his eyes are constantly rheumy. He looks neither right nor left, but softly wheezes and coughs, his eyes fixed on the ground as though he is an expert on soils and knows every foot of land in these parts.

On the other hand, the black dog had his eye on me. It seems that he must have taken a dislike to me from the very first. Whenever he saw me, he would growl deep in his throat and twitch his nostrils and lips. From time to time he would come over from the kvutzah, station himself in front of my fence, and bark, shaking his head as though he had a bone in his throat and couldn't get it out. He would growl at broken intervals, as much as to indicate that his barking was a form of questioning and he was going to go on and I was not going to chase him away.

After that he would run back to his master's dwelling, and I am certain that he would mount the terrace steps and lie down at the feet of the old man, gazing into his eyes as much as to say: Well, I have done all that is necessary for the moment.

I also noticed that the dog made things hard for himself by avoiding the little untended plot near the wood. In the morning the old gentleman went out for a nap among the trees. His black dog would frisk about in front of him, while the nurse would be carrying a sweater, a deck-chair and a little pillow. No sooner would the old man lie down and toilsomely arrange his exhausted limbs than the dog would turn round, and avoiding the untended patch, would go dashing off through the fields and hills and dales. In a little while he would come back, his sides rising and falling. He would rest his head in his master's lap and rub against him silently, as though fetching from distant places odors of healing herbs and vital essences to ease his master.

One night I heard a howling, the way dogs howl when the Black Angel descends upon an inhabited place. At that moment I happened to be sitting on a heap of pipes in my yard, rubbing my sick leg with my hand. When I heard the howling, my heart started within me. I got up and began running, limping toward the kvutzah. It was a clear blue night. The dog stood with his head pointing toward the sky.

The youngster on watch came quietly out of the shadow of the byre and asked: "Why are you running so? Has something happened over at your yard?"

"No," said I, breathing heavily and confused. "No, I heard the dog howling . . . and I was thinking that something . . . "

"No, nothing has happened."

When I came up to him, the dog ceased his howling. I saw that his mouth was open and he laughing, laughing at me and wagging his tail.

"Oho!" said I. "I must have fallen into a crazy sleep and had a dream."

As I spoke I bent down to pick up a stone, and fling it at the dog, but the watchman said to me:

"Let him be. This moon floating up in the sky is enough to make any living thing start howling and baying."

I lifted my eyes up to the moon. It was round, and it floated through the expanse of the heavens, trembling as though it was the white heart of the night.

"No," said I to the watchman, "I don't think it can make every living thing howl. It only raises the old question: Whence do you come and where do you stand and whither are you going?"

The watchman thought it over, then spat and asked:

"Well, and how about the account that has to be rendered?"

"Account to be rendered?" said I. "Yes, yes. Anyway, that new tenant of yours is probably hard at it now."

The watchman looked toward the dark windows of the house of the distinguished veteran, and shifted from foot to foot. "He has set aside a grave for himself up in the Galilee mountains," said he quietly. "He wants to be put away there, next to his wife's grave."

"Really?" said I in a weak voice.

"What's more, he is going to leave us and shift off somewhere else. It isn't pleasant for him here, for some reason."

The edge of my curiosity about the old veteran was dulled, and I went back to my own place. On the way I looked at the trees and saw that at night they lengthen and stand up straight, almost as though they had all turned into cypresses. I could not sleep and remained sitting in the open.

There was a vast oppressive silence across the whole horizon that left no space free. Only man speaks, said I to myself. Graves and stars are still. For a short while I sat, awake and not awake, then thought to myself again: Only man is silent; graves and stars speak.

In the morning I went to bed and slept till noon. After I had eaten, a large truck driven by Zalman entered the yard. Zalman is Rachel's brother, and sometimes the owners of my warehouse hire his truck. He never says anything to me, neither good nor bad. He never asks how I am and never tells me anything about his sister.

This time as well he came to take so many and so many pipes to town, and so much and so much wood. But to my astonishment, he didn't simply hand over the receipt for the stock lists to me as usual, but came up and said with a sullen face:

"I have a letter for you."

"A letter?"

He and his mate began to load up the truck while I vanished behind the warehouse. I didn't want them to see that my hands were trembling. I tore the envelope open and immediately saw that I had been foolish to suppose that it was a letter from Rachel. It was only a note from the owners of the warehouse containing instructions to give Zalman such and such amount of goods. But in addition they wished to inform me that they had decided to give up the warehouse, as the lease of the yard and the building was coming to an end. They had not yet made up their minds where they would transfer the business to, and could not know whether they would have any place for me.

I waited a few moments, then entered the building and stuck the letter on the small skewer on my table, which holds all my slips and receipts. I lit a cigarette and went back to the yard to supervise the loading. Zalman asked nothing and I said nothing. My eyes roamed the neighborhood, near and far, and all of a sudden, began to notice things they had never seen before. I noticed a large white road sign which had been simply invisible to me those many months. I realized that the distant hills had their backs turned to me. I understood that the days have an odor, not merely a color and a tone.

These discoveries kept me busy during the entire time that the truck was being loaded. Zalman climbed in, sat in the driver's seat, growled a goodbye to me and went off.

After the truck left the yard, I saw a stranger sitting in the shade of the building, his knapsack at his feet and his hat on the knapsack.

"Well now, how did you happen to drop in here? I didn't see you come at all."

"I traveled a stretch on that truck," said the stranger, smiling at me.

He was tall and lean, his hair was yellow and his cheeks were sunken. His Adam's apple wobbled in his throat and he had the sort of eyes you find in people who can see only one side of the coin.

"And what are you doing here?"

"I only came up to the Land a couple of days ago," said he, as though justifying himself, "and I've gone out to take a look at it. I walk a bit and ride a bit, I go from one place to another, and then I rest."

Why I suddenly felt happy I do not know.

"In that case, you can be my guest," said I quite emotionally, and slapped him on the shoulder. "By my faith, it's a long time since I have had a real guest."

He bared his yellowish teeth in a smile, and his ears moved back a little, too.

"I suppose you are hungry, eh?"

"Well, not too hungry," said he, shaking his head.

I took him to the tap and he washed his face while I provided him with soap and towel. Then I spread my mat in the shade of the trees, and fetched bread and olives and cheese and tomatoes and a jug of cold water out of the building. I dashed back and forth with no fear that this lad might be liable to get the wrong impression about the exaggerated hospitality of the Land. The guest came over, sat cross-legged and began eating with relish, while I sat facing him, jabbering without a break, just as though I was the newcomer and he the old-timer.

He slowly chewed with his yellow teeth, his Adam's apple moving up and down, while I talked to him, confusedly mixing everything up as though I were ploughing one furrow over another. I told him about my work, about the things that had happened to me in the Land and my inmost thoughts.

His mood became cheerful and he burst out laughing: "Why, it's almost as if I had known you for years and years!"

"Hahaha!" I laughed loudly in response.

"That's what they mean when they say that all Israel are brethren, eh?"

"Yes, yes, brethren," said I. "And now eat and don't be ashamed. Take a few more of the green olives!"

"Hohoho!" laughed the fellow, and his ears moved back.

"And what do you propose to do in the Land of Israel?"

"To do? I don't know. To begin with I propose to live here, just live . . . "

The pupils of his eyes dilated, as though at the

97

sudden apparition of a comet. So excited was he that he began to foam at the corners of his mouth, and his nose, which was peeling after a burn, wrinkled all over.

"Where are you going to settle down?"

"Oh, I don't feel like settling down yet. First of all I feel like going from place to place and seeing everything there is to see."

"I shan't be here for more than another few days either, for they are going to close this warehouse and I shall have to shift off somewhere else."

"Good!" said the lad. "And what if you do have to shift off somewhere else?"

I gathered up the leavings of his meal and put the food back. The sun began to decline in the west. The summits of the distant mountains became concave, as though preparing to catch and hold the drippings of the sunset.

The day's heat lessened a little, and the blue shirts in the fields looked like big flowers. A cow in heat lowed from the kvutzah yard, and the tortoise crawling slowly along the fence shrunk together and settled where he was, terrified by the noise.

The fellow turned his head toward Tel Hayyim and inspected it for a while. Then he shifted and got up.

"Well, thanks very much. Now I shall be getting along."

"Where to? What's the hurry? You can spend the night with me and go wherever you wish tomorrow. You can use my couch and be comfortable."

"And where will you sleep?"

"I mustn't sleep during the night hours, in any case. I am a watchman."

"No, no, I shall go to the kvutzah for the night.

They are pretty sure to make room for me there, and if they don't, I shall sleep in the open. I want to spend an evening at a kvutzah."

My delight left me as suddenly as it had come. I didn't stop to argue with him, but went along to see him on his way. He seemed to be dancing as he walked beside me, his knapsack on his shoulder and his thin shoulders hunched forward. He blinked his eyes at the blue horizon and said hoarsely: "Eh, there's a sky for you!"

After a brief silence he looked around at the un-tilled land covered with thorns and thistles, and ejaculated: "Eh, there's a land!" He shook his head from side to side and laughed to himself.

A sense of desolation took possession of me. I left him before he had gone halfway, and went back to my yard. I took the pitcher of water which was still standing outdoors and poured the contents over my little garden and the climbing vines on the fence. With nothing to do, I once again stretched out on my mat and began chewing a blade of some bitter grass. Haste was a thing that I did not particularly require—my possessions being few, my bundles light. I knew for certain that I could be easily uprooted and planted elsewhere, like any other dumb thing.

Yes, I knew how to be still as a dumb stone, to be still so long that even insects lost their fear of me. The air turned chilly, but I lay without moving, and the grapevine trellis above my head never moved either. One grape hung red there, a large bruised grape with a gray film. Drops of water from my pitcher which had sprayed around were trapped in the spider webs stretching between the leaves and the twigs.

A little spider came climbing up. She stood hesitant a moment, then descended circuitously; and in a moment a grape was linked to the fence by the finest of silver threads. In the middle of all her activity the spider suddenly took fright, gathered her limbs together and glided down. She must have been startled by the big fat fly which came trumpeting and swooping down. Or maybe she had not been startled at all, but was filled with joy at the sight of the tremendous prey which had come her way, and had lost control of herself in her great delight.

The black fly climbed up onto the grape and felt it. But a bee came along and drove him away. The sweet smell had deceived her as well. She came and sank her head in the grape as though it were a flower cup, but then realized her error and flew off. Finally a little insect turned up, of a kind I do not know. It had neither sting nor biting apparatus, and darted about until it reached the lip of the bruise. Instead of tasting the sweet abscess, it laid a tiny egg there, then another and yet another.

I suppose the insect had made a mistake, not having found the plant which serves as the repository of its seed. With the close of the day the hour of its death approached, and gloomy fear had led it to strew the fruit of its belly at random, here, there and anywhere. Or maybe this was no blind error at all, but one of the thousands of nature's tricks which are all included in the universal gestation.

My eyes had grown tired with their inspection of the works of creation. The day darkened and the horizon was a flaming fire. The kvutzah bell rang loudly, as though arousing people to put out the flames. I could feel my bad leg acting up. The pain was dull and irritating. I got up, lit the lamp in my room and got ready to go on watch.

All night long I did not sleep, lying down only at dawn. Scarcely had I fallen asleep when there was a knocking at my door. I got out of bed to open the door, and one of the Tel Hayyim lads burst in breathing heavily. He was barefoot and wore nothing but his trousers, and his hair was not yet combed.

"Listen, that visitor we had last night . . . You know him?"

"Dead?"

"He was sleeping in my room, and toward daylight he got up and asked for a drink of water, and when he went back to his bed he said he felt bad, and collapsed at once, and kept making a rattling noise in his throat until he became quiet."

"What? what? what?" I stammered as though stupefied.

"We've sent a messenger off on a horse to fetch the doctor, but I am afraid there is no hope." The fellow was very pale and kept hitching up his trousers all the time.

"Well, well, that such a thing could happen!"

"Tell me, didn't he spend a little time with you before he came to us?"

"Yes, he is a new arrival, he only came up to the Land a short while ago."

"And what's his name?"

"His name?"

Just think, I forgot to ask him for his name. For quite a while he and I had chatted about people and things and everything that was going on in the country, about the past and the future—and the only thing he did not tell me was his name.

"Or maybe you know where he comes from? Maybe he has kin or friends in the Land?"

"No, no, he has no kin or acquaintances. That I remember clearly."

"What's to be done? What's to be done?" muttered the fellow, scratching at his forehead. "There is nothing in his things, no passport or letter or notebook—nothing at all."

"Nothing at all?"

"How can a man leave on a journey and take nothing with him? I can't understand it."

I went over to Tel Hayyim with him, for all the world as though it were within my power to help. By the time we arrived the doctor had already completed his examination and had decided that the unknown fellow had died of apoplexy. There was a gloom all over the kvutzah. The women in charge of the little children gathered them together, while the young women looked at one another with dread in their eyes. The comrades pressed to the hut to look at the dead man's face, and all those stout lads were suddenly shaken and their faces turned gray.

The unknown lay on the bed, wearing an expression of calm and slight surprise. The kvutzah secretary entered and stood at his head, put his hands in his trousers pockets and pressed his lips together. He turned a fuming eye on me and grumbled:

"Such a mess! Now we shall have to take the horses from the fields and carry the body off to town."

"Why, why?" I asked, opposing him. "The poor fellow had just arrived in the Land, and it was just

102

his luck to have passed away in a kvutzah. Why do you have to send him off to be buried like a waif in some forsaken corner of a cemetery? Why don't you do him the last kindness and bury him here among you?"

"And what will you put on his grave?" asked one of the lads in a naive whisper. "Why, not one of us knows his name."

"That's no difficulty. Abraham the son of Abraham will be inscribed over his grave."

"Abraham the son of Abraham," the young fellow repeated after me, at a complete loss.

The three old men came to lay out the corpse, and sent the youngsters from the room. As I went out, from the other side of the window I heard one of the girls weeping, and saying:

"Oh, we don't know how to appreciate the little life that is given to us!"

I went back to my own place. I do not know what the Tel Hayyim comrades are going to do with their unknown dead. I hope they will take my advice and put him away here. It will mean that this evening a moist mound is going to rise in the untended patch, and in a day or two they may go out to fence it off and even put up a gravestone.

The day is still young. Calmly and slowly I begin putting my things together, and making an inventory of the warehouse. My heart is calm. When the time comes I shall go my way wherever it may be, and my traces will be forgotten in this place. But yonder, beside the young copse, a gravestone is going to rise, shining white against the green background. Henceforward this soil is going to know, to its very depths, that there's a small settlement standing here for good.

Darkness falls. I have finished my work, and I have all the time for myself. I gaze attentively at the stars, as though it is my duty to prepare an inventory of the heavens too. And now the night comes and spreads its wide blue wings. During the night it seems to me that I believe in God.

Most of Hono David's life I know only through the brief letters he used to send me when I was a young-ster. So it sometimes seems to me, when he comes to mind, that he himself never had any real life at all, and that from the very start he existed only in order to exert a certain effect on my own life.

Hono David was a kinsman of mine. He was a lean and long-armed lad with sunken eyes, a pointed chin, and a lofty, shining forehead. He had neither father nor mother, and so he lived together with us at grand-father's house in the little town. At first he attended the Heder, and then he took lessons from a teacher in the vernacular; but he was never much of a scholar and did not develop any taste for books. Instead, he had a passion for music. He bought himself a violin with the little money he had, and with his eyes closed under the surge of his emotions he would make a medley on it of the songs to be heard in the sur-rounding villages, or else he would play the tunes the blind fiddlers fiddled on market days.

Grandfather, the head of the house and a man of standing, used to fling bitter words at him. A big fel-low like he was, he used to say, ought to open his eyes instead of shutting them tight. Here it is a great big world spreading far and wide, all of it calling for ac-tion, and instead this fellow has to go and get stuck in nonsense for which there was only a very dim future. Either study or work; that is the only alternative before a man in Israel, and happy is he who can sit at both tables! But to do neither the one nor the other, just to "stretch out over empty space and hang over nothing"—what sense was there in that?

While speaking, grandfather would look at Hono David with those gray eyes of his, which would have been utterly icy were it not for the rheum of old age floating in them and tempering their severity. Hono David would stand before him looking at the floor, swinging his long arms just a trifle while the fingers of his left hand moved as though he were plucking invisible strings.

Once he was no longer permitted to play in the house he would vanish into the byre at the end of the courtyard, where he would scrape and saw away in the gloom amid the smells of hay and cattle dung, while the chickens roosted in a row on the sloping beams and peered at him slantwise. Every week grandfather used to set out on his tour of the villages and the estates of the "gentry." Those were days of freedom for Hono David, who would promptly take his violin and proceed to the Catholic church. In the tiny dwelling of the organist he diligently devoted himself to the study of music, practicing the best pieces and patiently putting up with the whims of his teacher. The organist was a dwarfish, weakly man, with a mustache that fluttered like the wings of a big moth. All day long he drank himself drunk and staggered about with bloodshot eyes, bellowing at the top of his voice, his mouth constantly cursing and vilifying. But between one fit of swearing and the next the spirit would rest upon him, his soul be purified, so to speak, and he would enlighten his pupil, who stood before him in fear and awe.

A long time passed in this fashion. I was a boy of about twelve, and Hono David was about five years or more older. Whenever grandfather's rebukes oppressed him he would come and sit down by me, rest his slender hands on my table, gaze at them and smile. He did not strike up any friendships with the young fellows of the town, I being the only one he regarded as a comrade. It was quite clear to me that he was entirely out of step; a young fellow like him would soon be ready to stand under the bridal canopy, but his legs were not in the least familiar with the ways of the world. Yet this passionate ravenous hunger which possessed him, the rare spirit which throbbed within him, filled my heart with a vast pride; and after an intimate conversation with him I would find it hard to go back to comrades of my own age, who were tussling and wrestling on the ground, and racing pigeons.

On one occasion Hono David plucked up the courage to go to grandfather and ask to be sent to one of the big towns in order to study at a musical conservatory. It was at twilight, when grandfather was accustomed to walk about alone in the parlor, his hands clasped behind his back, talking to himself. His muffled voice would rise from time to time behind the closed door, and I could never make out whether he was casting up the accounts of his business or of his life. That was a very uncertain time of day indeed. Sometimes grandfather would rest his hand on your head, and merely by doing so would bring you a sense of gentle mercy and pity; as though the sunset hues on the horizon had gathered into your heart. You would be prepared to vow that henceforward you would indeed be good and do good to all—yet not know why.

But sometimes grandfather would stand still in front of you without touching you, his eyes wandering and alien, the tassels of his girdle continuing to shake as though they could see some unclean thing in you; then you and your requests would fade away all of a sudden, your lips would droop in your perplexity, and your feet would grow weak. Something of that kind was what happened to Hono David. Grandfather looked at him without answering a word, merely put out his hand and straightened Hono David's coat lapel, blew a little feather from his shoulder and fixed his crooked cap. Then he went back to pacing up and down the room, after his measured fashion.

Hono David never asked him for anything else again. Thenceforward a new idea began to take shape within him, and during the long winter evenings he told me what had occurred to him. He intended to get up one night and run away from the town, feeling quite certain that nobody would regret it in the least. For what was the good of hanging around and just being in the way at home? He would go from town to town, earning money with his violin, until he found what he wanted. It was not clear to me whether he wished to settle down in some spot where there were great musicians and he could study properly, or whether he merely intended to go wandering about the world for his personal pleasure and profit. But I did not trouble to inquire too deeply into what was beyond me. The truth was that I did not believe he would do what he said, for never in my life had I seen Hono David actually do anything. But the fantasy itself was sufficient to sustain one's spirit during those dull evenings amid the wastes of snow and wind that howled in the chimney. I responded to Hono David and entered wholeheartedly into his secret; and for long hours the two of us, the young man and the lad, would sit together leaning over the table, whispering, and weaving the threads of many a mystery.

The map of the world was spread out before us. Our fingers ran across the green patches which represented the plains of Europe, leaping over the rich brown cinnamon of heights and mountain chains, and sailing across the blue of the seas and oceans. Like the linkmen of the town, who went about with torches in their hands as evening fell and, with a single touch, kindled the light in the street lamps one after the other, so we would linger at the tiny circles on the map above which could be seen the names of the large cities. We would fix our eyes on them for a moment and would promptly see before us the magnificent visions of noisy streets, electric signs, and lively crowds. For us each town's name was a kind of seed secreted in the soil of the future, from which would grow a majestic tree. It was as if the gates of the world had opened, and at the main crossroads stood Hono David, jubilant and exultant, preparing to stride forward with manly steps. Sometimes he would suspend his travels across the map, and with his finger fixed somewhere between Great Britain and the Bay of Biscay would begin dreaming aloud of the splendors hidden in the distance, and of the web of life which was to be, and woven entirely of music and delight.

Here, to be sure, I was after all just an onlooker, yet in spite of this my heart moaned and my eyes grew moist. Hono David, seeing this, took pity on me, and rose and swore that whenever he arrived at a new spot he would remember me and send me a picture postcard together with brief greetings, since he did not like to write long letters. And in order that I might know whether fortune had smiled upon him, he would draw a flag in the margin of the postcard. If the flag were white, it would be a sign that things were going well with him and his fortune favored him. This proposal seemed very sound indeed to me, since it added color to the great secret.

All that winter long Hono David hoarded his pennies. He found a small suitcase in a storeroom, and in it he placed his underwear and the good clothes he had prepared and patched. When spring came, a few weeks after Passover he vanished from the house in the dead of the night. That last evening he spent in my room with me as usual, remaining until midnight. He no longer gazed at the map of the world, but sat pinching his chin distractedly, meditating and then rousing himself afresh every few moments to gaze round about him as though he wished to engrave the objects and their shadows on his memory.

It used to be my habit to stay up late reading in bed, and so I would keep the lamp burning in my room till very late. Only after I had fallen asleep would one of the family come and turn it out. But that evening I could not master my drowsiness, and I fell fast asleep while Hono David sat silently beside me. When I woke up in the morning, all traces of him had already vanished. The family looked at each other in great wonder and could not understand what had happened. All eyes turned to me, and naturally I found myself in the center of the affair for the time being, my importance quite magnified. Grandfather was not at home, and I trembled for fear that he should flare up on account of the scandal, and set out to chase the runaway and bring him back home "like a vessel full of shame"; in which case, all the thread of action which had been spun in my room during the winter nights would be swept away like so much cobweb.

The following evening, when grandfather came back, I planted myself in front of him with trembling knees before he had taken off his dust coat or could put his walking stick away in a corner, and with leaden tongue I started telling him the tale in fragmentary fashion. Grandfather was taken aback. His mouth fell open a trifle and his beard began quivering. The stern authority of his face melted away, and a troubled wrinkle of concern appeared on his forehead. Could such a thing really happen in *his* household? How would he be able to walk about among folk henceforward, and how would he look to people? Looking at him, my heart ached within me and I shared his grief. Had I been able, I would have turned back the wheel of time and uprooted the event.

"But what of it?" said the family, as though washing their hands of the matter. "Hono David has already come of age, and surely he knows what he is about." Grandfather however went to the window, still wearing his mantle and holding his stick; and for quite a while he stood there silently tapping his fingers on the pane.

Grandfather did not set out in pursuit of the runaway, and folk did not criticize him much for not doing so. Hono David had indeed been right in his estimate. He had taken himself off and departed like a temporary guest, leaving no gap behind. But I, young as I was, began to await his letters impatiently. Our little town did not have a postman to go the rounds of the houses. Instead, the residents went to the post office three times a week. There at a stated hour, the clerk would come to the door, call out the names of those who had received letters and newspapers, and distribute them. I also now began going to the post office regularly three times a week; and there I would stand to one side, confused and humble. We heard rumors that Hono David spent some time wandering about the small towns and villages of the neighborhood, playing his violin at weddings and on festival occasions. Apparently he must have come to the conclusion that there was no point in sending off letters from nearby places, and so had decided to wait until he crossed the frontier and found himself in another country.

But one day I heard my name being called by the postal clerk, an albino with curly hair, an open Jewhater who had his own private revenge on the Jews by systematically mispronouncing their names. My heart leaped up, and I began to blush at all the eyes that were turned on me. The clerk twisted my name about a second time, and since I still remained dumb, a number of fingers pointed at me and sev-

eral voices cried in unison: "Here he is! Here he is!"
From hand to hand over all their heads the first of
the letters of Hono David was passed to me. I could
no longer control myself and behave properly, and
with burning eyes I turned and dashed away.

When I came home I called out tremulously:

"Grandfather, this is Hono David writing! He is
already over the frontier!"

Grandfather stopped his walk, clasped his hands
behind him, and growled into the air: "We shall
live and see! We shall indeed live and see!"

The letter was exceedingly brief. It was a picture
postcard with a view of a city, a spacious square with
a leaping fountain of water. There were carriages
standing in the shade of trees along an avenue, and
passers-by lifting one foot, as though it had been
scorched and they never intended to put it down
again; just as though the whole of that city had
turned to stone for a moment when my kinsman
Hono David came along with his violin under his
arm. The other side of the card flaunted two or three
rows of large disjointed letters. But in the margin
there was a modest little white flag—and that was
the most important thing. Thank God! Thank God!
Hono David was well and in a cheerful frame of
mind.

The postcards began to arrive one after the other,
all short and to the point, each of them with a white
flag in the margin. White flags fluttered to me from
all over Europe, and signaled: "All's well, all's well!"
A rich and peaceful world stretched far and wide,
like a green pasture rich with food and quiet contentment. Most of Hono David's messages resem-
bled one another and so did the pictures on the

postcards. He had little to tell of what happened to him and never described his way of living. It seemed that he was always in haste when he kept the promise he had made me; as though he felt it a pity to turn his eyes away even for a brief moment from the varying landscapes and colorful life all around him. But I would immerse myself in the few lines he wrote, obstinately going over them again and again and drawing whatever information I could from the very shape and the very flourishes of the letters. Yet the only foundation I had for my guesses was the white flag. As long as this signaled from afar, it meant that Hono David was content and was making the world a happier place.

At first he used to send me two postcards a week. Later, there began to be long intervals between one card and the next. Finally he reached one of the large capitals of Europe in the course of his wanderings, and ceased to write. I said to myself: Probably the fellow has reckoned up his affairs and feels it his duty to pitch himself a stake somewhere in the world. Maybe he has found some sort of steady living and has settled down to devote himself to the study of music, as he has so long wanted to do. Or maybe he has fitted himself into the pattern of everyday life, leaving all his former dreams far behind him, and no longer feels it was the proper thing for him to send letters to a boy in some Godforsaken little town, or to play about with white flags. He knew all about white flags and had nothing fresh to tell. If that was the case—let him make the most of it and have a good time. I certainly had nothing against him!

A long time passed and the travels of Hono David lost their wonderful zest. Sometimes I would turn up at the post office, but there were no longer any great expectations in my heart. The map of the world in my room had once again become a flat sheet of paper covered with dots and splashes of color with no life or mystery about them.

A year and a half passed. I was still in grandfather's house. I had been accepted as a member of the Hashahar Zionist Society and participated in meetings, in fund-raising and in choruses which sang the Zionist songs. But that was not enough for me, and in my solitary hours I would turn my thoughts to my future. I began fearfully to feel that I was late; that I had to hurry and cross life's threshold while the door was open; otherwise it might be closed and locked, God forbid, and I would never find it open again. I would argue back and forth with myself: You have nothing to show for your life, and you would not have the strength to rise up and revolt against your fate as Hono David did. His days must surely be flowing like proud streams into the great sea; while your days are like a spring puddle in your town, which ends by turning green and drying up.

Spring passed. The days began to wear the colors of summer. The few lilacs in front of my window began to fade. There were glorious moonlit nights, but my concern about my future stuck like a thorn in my soul. I began to wake up during the night, at that late hour when even the nightingale has ceased its singing. There was a still silence all over the world which seemed to be waking me up from time to time.

My room would assume an unfamiliar shape. A huge shadow seemed to stand at the door, as though it had come to demand what I owed it. Sometimes

I would put my head out of the window and gaze at the heart of the night, wondering: What must I do? The empty square in the heart of the little town was as clean as though it had just had a bath, and there was not a sign of dirt or muck. The smell of the grass reached me from hidden places, and in the sky the stars blinked their lids. I would gaze at the moon and it would gaze back at me, as though both of us were waiting for the same thing, but did not know what it was.

Then one day quite unexpectedly a letter arrived from Hono David. This time it was actually a letter, a sheet of paper which had been placed in an envelope with the address "Jerusalem" on top. Never before had a letter from the Land of Israel been received in our town; and it came to me, the youngest and least of the members of Hashahar, and furthermore it was a kinsman of my own who, it seemed, was actually there, having set up his tent between the sea and the mount of the Lord. All the patrons of the post office came crowding around me, just as though a letter sent from the Land of Israel was public property and it was obvious that I should stand in the middle of the market square and read it aloud to everybody.

The news took wing. On my way home Jews were already peeping out at me from their shop doorways as though they could smell the fields of Galilee. I suddenly assumed stature in the eyes of the comrades who happened to be with me; and before I had even a chance of reading the letter to myself, I had already been instructed to come to the club room that evening and present a full report, on the basis of the trustworthy testimony of Hono David.

It was a long letter, which was quite unlike Hono David. He informed me that by chance he had met a Jew who had made money overseas but whose children were incensed against him in his old age, so that he had become alienated from them. And since the old man had nothing left in life he had fallen into a deep despondency, and had finally decided to retire from business and take his ease in some sunny spot. He had picked on Hono David and hired him to accompany him as a kind of combination secretary-attendant, and play to him when the mood was upon him. Hono David had supposed that they would be going to one of the health resorts that rich folk favor, but had found in the end that he was in error. Maybe the old man wanted to put some distance between himself and his heirs, or maybe he had other reasons which were hidden in the depths of his heart. But anyway, he went off one day and traveled to the Land of Israel with Hono David, and went up to Jerusalem with him.

Hono David never had had anything to do with Zion and had never even troubled to consider Israel's relations with the other nations, Jerusalem had been outside his field of vision. When fate brought him there he appears to have become confused. And so he wrote in his letter: "Jerusalem—do you call this a city? Here there is nothing to be found but mountains and mountains, and a dumb soul wandering about among them. What is there here for a flesh-and-blood human being to come looking for?"

To him Jerusalem seemed to be a kind of broken violin, and he was astounded that so many generations should have played the melody of redemption on that particular cracked instrument. "We are lodging in a gloomy inn," he wrote, "and ever since we have come here my old patron has sealed his lips, as though he has taken a vow of silence. I cannot find out how long he proposes to remain, but I am very grateful to him because he does not require me to play. I tune the strings from time to time, but they are not yet properly tuned. It seems to me that the four strings of my violin are no longer enough."

Hono David had never written before in this fashion. For him his violin had been one of his chief limbs, which there was no disputing. If he now wrote about himself and his violin, it was a sign that his cup was full to overflowing. And since he did not have at his disposal the words he required to express himself, he suddenly ended his letter, and under his signature drew a black flag drooping feebly and hanging to one side.

The black patch at the end of the letter depressed me even more than the outspoken words within it. It was like a reed stuck into the sea, round which a sandbank had gathered. A fault had developed in the strata of existence. The whole world rested safe in the shadow of white flags, and Jerusalem alone was flapping her black flag at me from her heights. At that moment I felt like someone seeing a small cloud appear in the blue sky on a fine day.

I entered the house and quietly announced: "Hono David is in Jerusalem!" Grandfather was sitting in the big armchair, his long pipe in his mouth. When he heard my words he let the pipestem go for a moment, and gazed at me in silence. What a grandfather he is! said I to myself, see how stony he has made his heart! Just look, even a letter from the

Holy Land does not soften him. I went to my room and read the letter over a second and third time, and mused upon its gloominess.

I had a corner between the closet and the cupboard where I kept all the things I prized, including the letters of Hono David, all arranged in their proper sequence and tied together by a scarlet thread. I added this fresh letter to the bundle which I put back in its place.

That evening I did not join my comrades at the club. I did not have the heart to go and cloud over all those bright eyes, which would be shining at me in the hope that I would bring them a picture of blue and white, of sunrise over the mountains of Judea, of climbing vines and creeping vines and heaping sheaves of corn, of grapevines and fig trees and those who dwell beneath them.

That night I could not sleep. The lamp burned on my table as usual, and I lay in my bed while pulsating visions passed before my eyes.

Late at night the door opened and grandfather entered my room. I thought he had come to put out the lamp, so I pretended to be asleep. But between my eyelids I watched and saw him hesitate a moment, approach the corner between the closet and the cupboard, and take out Hono David's letter from the pile. He removed the latest letter from its place, looked at the address on top and murmured to himself: "Jerusalem! Yes, he really is in Jerusalem!"

He turned to the light, held the letter at arm's length before his eyes after the fashion of old folk, and read it from beginning to end. For the first time it suddenly became apparent to me that he had indeed grown old. He stooped and his hands trembled a little, and he no longer gave the impression of being one solid piece.

In a little while he turned around and very quietly put the bundle back in the corner, took up the lamp, and left the room on tiptoe.

Time passed and once again nothing was heard from Hono David. I used to wonder what could have happened to him in Jerusalem, and whither fate had taken him from there. Grandfather changed his behavior and three times a week would silently turn his eyes to me. Sometimes he would even ask in so many words: "Well, and what else do they write to you?" All I could do was shrug my shoulders and bend up my arms. I did not reveal that I had witnessed his strange conduct in my room that night, and I took care to disregard the slight change that had taken place in him. When at length another letter arrived from Hono David, I kept myself in check and did not open it at the post office, but brought it home still sealed and handed it over to grandfather. He did not take it but signaled and said: "Open it and read it aloud."

This time we learned that Hono David was still in Jerusalem. To his misfortune his patron had had a sudden heart attack, and died in that same miserable inn where they had been staying. The consul of the country from which the old man came refused to give any help to Hono David, since he was a native of another land, and so he was left alone and penniless. "Never in all my life have I known such loneliness as I am experiencing in Jerusalem," wrote Hono David. "It seems to me that I must have made some great mistake in my life, though I do not know what it can have been. I suddenly find myself old. Maybe it is my lot to remain here motionless, like those stones, and that ages and epochs should pass over my head. Maybe it is my lot to grow a beard and wear a long colored robe like the other Jews here; to rest my head against the stones of the Wailing Wall and to wait for I don't know what."

This letter did not carry any drawing of a flag at all.

A week later a short letter arrived. It was the last letter to come from Hono David. I remember that evening was beginning to fall. The odors of a fruitful land were wafted through the air. The blue of the skies was becoming gradually deeper, and there was a delicate luminescence along the horizon. Children could be heard at their carefree play in the street.

And this is what the letter said: "Tomorrow I am leaving here. I want to go back home. If grandfather will receive me, I shall start all over again. I have sold everything I have and all the belongings of the dead old man, and so I have enough for the journey. If it should be necessary, I shall also sell the violin; but I doubt whether anybody will give me much money for it."

When I finished reading the short letter to grandfather, he stood up, buttoned up his robe, took his stick in his hand, and left the house, just as though Hono David had already reached the gate of the town and was waiting at the crossroads below the hill, where the image of the crucifix stood under a small board hut facing the sunrise. The family sat down to drink tea, and the samovar hissed and muttered. I sat crouched in that special corner of my room, undid the string around Hono David's bundle of letters and read them through in reverse order, beginning with the last, until I once again reached the pictures of the distant capitals frozen in their first bloom, and the white flags which had fluttered so joyously in their time, only to fade and be furled so suddenly.

I pictured the course of Hono David's life as a circle, the circle a snake makes biting its tail. I felt a mixture of joy and grief: joy because Hono David would return and tell me, alone, all that had happened to him in colorful detail; grief because he would return to the place from which he had started and would have nothing to show. He would forsake the paths of Zion and would come back to walk the rutted and unpaved streets of the town, as colorless as he had been at the beginning, as though he had spent all his time in vain.

When night fell grandfather came back from the market. From my room I heard him, putting his stick away in a corner, setting his hat on the cupboard and donning a skullcap. Then he remarked casually and at random: "War has been declared!"

The samovar was still humming. The children were still shouting and calling in the street. Darkness slowly descended on the world. From a corner in my room I seemed to see far, far away, a skull floating upon huge seas; Hono David struggling desperately with the last remnants of his strength to get back home.

But he never returned again. All trace of him has been lost to this very day.